MW01234591

LOVE

WITHOUT

BOUNDARIES

LOVE WORKED OUT WHEN

NO ONE EXPECTED

This is a work of fiction. Names, character, places and incidents are either the product of the author's imagination or are used fictitiously, and any resemblance to actual persons, living or dead, business establishments, events or locales is entirely coincidental.

@ COPYRIGHT 2023 BY (CHRISTOPHER WOODWARD)

CHAPTER 1

Mom recommended that I visit my aunt's home in the hills while I was on summer leave from college. Although legally my aunt, she was my mom's younger cousin sister and not much older than me. She used to visit the ancestral home of our grandfather while she was on her summer break, which was the same as when we were. She indulged me to the max, playing with me, telling me stories, feeding me delicious food she had prepared, and even putting me to sleep. I enjoyed having her around.

Even after all these years, I could still remember her signature scent sweeping across me as I dozed off in her lap. That was the most vivid childhood memory I could recollect. Her visits ceased after she began attending college, and we lost contact when her father was transferred up north. She had gotten married about a year ago, but I couldn't go because of my exams.

She had had a personal tragedy six months prior when the ship her husband was stationed on vanished in a storm and was never found. She was expecting at the time, and the shock had led to a miscarriage, but she had handled it bravely, refusing any assistance and remaining alone on the remote farm up in the mountains where they had settled.

She had invited the entire family to come visit her, but none of us could make it because of other commitments and the fast-paced nature of life. When I returned from the holidays, Mom asked me if I would like to go because I was her favorite. I leaped at the possibility for a trip to cool off before returning to my books because I was tired of the heat.

So plans were made and tickets were purchased for a two-week engagement with my childhood idol. Hearing the excitement in her voice over the phone made whatever worries I may have had about seeing her after all these years go. I could hardly get a word in edgeways because of my reserve. After that, my mother teased me mercilessly about the innocent comments I had made when I was younger about marrying her when I grew up, which made me flush in shame.

Because of my excitement, the sound of her voice, the tinkling laughter, and the smell of her perfume, which brought back memories of my childhood, I was unable to sleep that night. After all these years, I wondered if she would still recognize me and vice versa. I was no longer a boy, and she was now a married woman. I was worried that the carefree informality we enjoyed would vanish. I was worried that it would be replaced by an awkwardness that would be made worse by my natural reserve.

She was the only girl I had ever spoken to; I tend to be quiet and awkward around people of the opposite sex. I doubted myself once more and came close to withdrawing after wondering if it was a mistake to say yes. But, the joy in her speech caused me to reconsider and set my reservations aside. It would be good to put a grin back on her face—a face that had brought me great delight and had previously been weighed down by a mountain of problems—if I could just temporarily restore her happiness.

So I set off on a voyage that would take me farther than I had ever imagined it would, with a sense of expectation, mixed with a dash of anxiety, and conflicting emotions raging in my mind. Mom insisted on packing homemade treats and supplies for the trip, making me feel as though I were going on an adventure into an uncharted desert. I was left with nothing except a backpack, which I barely managed to fit my clothes and other essentials. In addition to the food, which could feed an army, there were plenty of instructions and suggestions. I embarked on what would turn out to be the biggest adventure of my life without fully realizing the profound impact that a hasty choice may have.

She.

The previous year had been an emotional roller coaster, with highs of feeling on top of the world and lows of seeing your dreams dash to pieces all around you. Up in the hills, experiencing the pleasures of wedded bliss and surviving mostly on love and fresh air, I had a dream wedding and a wonderful beginning to married life. When I discovered that I was in the family way and that our love had produced fruit, our joy had no bounds.

Yet, it was offset by the melancholy of his leaving because his shore leave had come to an end and he had to report back to work. He had assured me that he would return to see the birth of our child, so I didn't worry. I had no idea that the final goodbye kiss I gave him would be the last one. That would be the last I ever saw of him, in a horrible turn of events that magnified life's vicissitudes, and it would leave a gaping wound where my heart once beat.

I still clearly recall that day, as I was working in the kitchen and humming a song to our unborn child, when the phone rang. The moment I heard those words from the other side, my entire world began to spin, and I fell to the ground in a heap.

When I regained consciousness, I discovered myself laying in a pool of blood with a severe abdominal discomfort. I called for help in a haze and spent the following week in the hospital, broken at the loss of both my kid and my spouse in the span of one day.

His ship had become mired in a storm and vanished off the face of the earth. I had lost all desire to life and had turned numb and emotionless. When they found out about the catastrophe, my family members who had raced to my side begged me to go back to my farm with them, but I was adamant about doing so.

My mother wanted to go with me and stay with me to support me through it, but I wouldn't hear of it. To confront my inner demons, come to grips with them, and accept my loss, I had to go through it alone. Despite the fact that I genuinely lacked the desire to live any longer, I didn't want my immediate family to even have a hint of the misery I was going through.

I was going through the motions like a zombie with no joy for anything since the winter had stripped away all the color from my life. Even the tears would not come; there was a void, a dull anguish that made me feel as though I were being torn apart.

CHAPTER 2

They were dark times, and I let myself go, not caring at all about how I looked or how I interacted with people.

Even though I seemed to be fine, my parents used to contact me every day out of concern for my welfare. When they found I wasn't, they made me swear at the very least to take care of my nutrition and health. Then, something deep within of me awoke, forcing me to snap out of my melancholy if not for family, then at least for me. I got myself together, back into shape, and started working with a fury because I didn't want to give myself time to be depressed.

I didn't have time to grieve, but there was still sadness inside of me. The cold nights were especially painful because it was hard to fall asleep by myself because I missed his warm body next to mine and the pleasures of the flesh to which my body had grown accustomed. Dreams of his ravenous appetite and tender touches would cause me to awaken in a hot flush, wet, and in need of satisfaction.

In order to relieve the pain in my breasts, which had been fairly painful and full, I had to express my milk. I got in touch with the neighborhood hospital and offered my assistance with a baby milk bank.

After a protracted slumber, the snow thawed and the first green shoots emerged, signaling the beginning of a season of rebirth and optimism. When I received an unexpected call from my cousin, I was already feeling overwhelmed by the sheer number of activities that needed to be completed. She asked if I would mind if her son, who was home for the holidays, came to see me for a fortnight before starting college.

It brought back a lot of pleasant memories from when I was younger and carefree, spending every summer at our grandfather's place. My favorite of her children, I enjoyed thinking back on those enjoyable times spent eating, playing, and enjoying myself. As he maintained he would only marry me, I remember how embarrassed I would flush. Despite the taunting I received from the family, it would be so lovely to be adored.

Since I hadn't seen him in a long time, I wasn't sure if he would even recognize me. After a season full of monosyllabic discourse, I was so ecstatic that I was yakking nonstop as if I were dying to let all the words out that were almost overflowing. He picked up the phone and gave his mother a hesitant hello before hanging up. It seemed like spring had finally arrived because for the first time in months, I had something to look forward to. My head was bursting with delight as it made its way to my lips. While I danced around the house completing chores that no longer seemed like an insurmountable burden, I noticed that I was humming a song. In the few days before his arrival, there was a lot of work that needed to be done to have everything back in working order, but I didn't mind; in fact, I was anxiously anticipating it and counting down the days until he arrived.

I took off my clothes that evening and looked at myself in the mirror for the first time since that tragic day. Although I had neglected myself, I didn't look half awful as I practiced a come hither while striking a variety of stances, some sensual and some seductive.

I was even dripping between my legs from that stare. I was glowing like a newlywed before her honeymoon.

My face had regained its vigor, my eyes were flashing with glee, and a smile was playing on my lips despite the need for a trim on my untamed hair. Even though it was cold outside, my skin was warm and covered in a multitude of goose bumps all over its smooth surface—more from anticipation than from the cold. My nipples were protruding from the deep pink areola like nubs, and my breasts had really filled up. My tummy had fat rolls lower down that highlighted my adorable navel in the middle. Moving down, my slit was surrounded by untamed tendril jungles that might use some major gardening. My bottom was round and smooth, and my hips were mature and curved. After getting my nails done, my thighs were toned and tapered down to my smooth knees, muscular calves, and killer feet.

I still had the charm to entice them in and I looked too good to resist. I simply struggled with the question of whether having such sexual fantasies was appropriate. As he was my cousin's son, I should have been a bereaved widow, but I reminded myself that loving oneself is not sinful.

I was as busy as a bee the next three days getting everything back in order, especially myself.

The home appeared habitable again the day before he arrived, so I started taking good care of myself. After giving my hair a trim, I gave myself a nice massage with almond oil, massaging it into my skin and opening every pore as I savored the rekindled sensual and feminine feelings that I had thought had long since died and gone.

I removed any remaining hair from my armpits and concentrated on removing the overgrowth that covered my loins. My treasure pot, which had been veiled from view, gradually came back into focus. Suddenly, my mound was as smooth as a baby, and I felt ten years younger and virginal as before. My lips were moist as my fingers delved into the warm depths of my bud, which was moving as I massaged it.

I closed my eyes and let the warm water flow over my body as I thought back to the night of my wedding, when I changed from a girl to a woman. My fingers mimicked his internal movements as I expanded like a flower in blossom. My body began to tremble as months of suppressed sexuality suddenly sprang to the surface because I was in such desperate need of relief. I imagined him making me whole and cradling me in his arms once more as I orgasmed. After taking a lavish bath, I gave myself some more self-love and went to bed for the first time in months. I awoke the next morning feeling rejuvenated and like a brand-new person.

I immediately got to work, whipping up his favored supper. After taking a bath, I put on my favorite saree and, for the first time in six months, opened my cosmetics bag. I applied kohl, rouge, perfume, and lip gloss, looking more alluring than ever and confident that my charms were still intact—if anything, they were stronger than ever. If appearances could kill, a whole army would fall dead at my feet in a flash. With that knowledge in hand, I walked up and down in anticipation of his arrival.

He.

After a day-long train trip, I took a bus for a few hours to the closest town in the hills, where I caught a cab for the final hour's drive to her property, which was hidden away in the highlands and about 40 kilometers distant. The clear, chilly mountain air was invigorating. Whatever reservations or concerns I had were completely dispelled. I closed my eyes and tried to recall dim memories of my youth spent with her from my memory bank.

Before I left for my trip, Mom had called me at least a dozen times to check on me and make sure everything was alright. I felt a little upset, but I realized it was only a motherly worry that never goes away. She had given me specific directions to her home and cautioned me that the Wi-Fi and signal in the isolated area of the mountain could be spotty, but I wasn't a kid anymore.

I went back in time more than ten years to try to piece together my patchwork of recollections, some of which were crystal clear and others fuzzy. She used to go by Dipa, and I went by Krishna. Her oiled hair was pulled back into pigtails with a red ribbon at the end. She was wearing a skirt and a top, and she had glass bracelets on her wrists. Her eyes were so sweet, and she had a grin on her lips all the time. I mainly thought about those things.

CHAPTER 3

When Mom wasn't carrying me, I would follow her everywhere like a tiny lamb. Nobody else mattered while she was around because she would treat me like a baby, feeding me with her own hands and saving the best bites and treats just for me. I would sleep in her lap in the sweltering afternoons as she told me delightful stories that enthralled me, and she insisted on bathing me while I blushed at the memory of her seeing me in the nude. I would put my hand in her sleeve as I curled up next to her warm body at night while we slept together, feeling safe and secure in her embrace.

The cab arrived at its destination, came to a stop, and the sudden interruption jolted me out of my daydream. When I heard my name being called, she was waving to me while wearing a stunning maroon saree. I was astounded by the sight of beauty that appeared to me out of the mist. She hurried over to me and tightly hugged me as I unloaded the bags and paid the payment.

When she hugged me, I felt a little awkward because I wasn't a child anymore but was immediately taken back in time. The grin and the eyes remained the same, but I could see that they carried a hint of sadness. But now that she had gained weight and developed the most incredible curves, she looked so stunning that even a supermodel would be ashamed.

I could smell her distinctive scent again as she wrapped her arms around me, but it had a somewhat more mature flavor, which caused me to close my eyes as I breathed it in. Despite my best attempts, I couldn't help but feel a hard on coming up, so I took a step back before she noticed and called me a pervert.

She asked me why I was so silent, but she was talking so much that I couldn't respond. As I replied that she rarely gave me a chance to open my mouth, it delighted me to hear her tinkling laughing. Despite my objections, she insisted on carrying the enormous bag that my mother had filled with the supplies as we walked the kilometer to her farm over hillside pathways.

She.

While I was eagerly and anxiously expecting his arrival, I refrained from calling him because I figured his mother had probably already made enough calls for the entire extended family. In order to save him the trouble of trying to find my farm, I made the decision to meet him at the main road and informed him when I arrived there in plenty of time.

This was the first time I had left the house since leaving the hospital, and I thought what a terrifying sight I would have made—a woman decked out to the nines driving down a deserted mountain road—straight out of one of those ghost stories we girls used to swap at late-night sleepovers to terrify the living daylights out of one another.

My thoughts drifted back a decade to our final summer spent together at our village home as I sat down on a boulder. As the only child in the family, I treasure the holidays spent with my cousins at my grandparents' house. I was the youngest of them all, and the next youngest was at least 12 years older than I was. They were all married when I was still in school, and we didn't have anything in common other than our common lineage, so I felt a little out of place.

But, the only reason I was looking forward to those days was spending time with Krishna, as I had no need of anything or anyone else. He was the only one who was even remotely my age, and he utterly captivated me. He consumed my entire day, to the point that I became quite possessive of him and wouldn't even let his mother near him. Although he was still a toddler, I pondered whether he remembered anything of those times. I also attempted to picture how much he would have changed and whether he would still be recognizable to me and vice versa.

A few meters away, a car stopped, and a muscular young man came out to unload the luggage. Despite the fact that his size had altered and he was no longer a waif I could carry in my arms (probably the reverse would hold true with a physique toned and muscled, like a Greek God). Even at a distance of a mile, I could instantly recognize that unruly mop of hair, those sharp eyes, and that timid smile. I chastised myself for having such silly thoughts. I hurried toward him in my saree, disregarding all manners and how ridiculous I must have appeared, because I was so eager to see him again after such a long time. I gave him a tight hug and was about to kiss him when I noticed that he had slightly backed away. I'm glad I restrained myself since I would have felt embarrassed.

I struggled to contain my tears as I gave him a hug, and I could tell he was experiencing the same thing. When I'm under pressure, I have this bad habit of talking nonstop to keep my mind off of whatever worry it may be feeling. I started babbling, my six months of silence increasing my verbosity allotment.

He wasn't expecting a storm to hit him with such fury, and he was dumbfounded and confused. I initially assumed that he was following me because he wanted me to take the lead, but a quick glance behind him revealed that he was actually inspecting my behind. I grinned to myself, choosing to keep it a secret rather than make things any more awkward than they already were. He stole a glimpse my direction with an expression I couldn't quite place before hurriedly averting his eyes when they met mine.

Then it dawned on me that my Krishna was no longer a youngster and appeared to be a little taken in by my charms. He was an upgraded beta version in my opinion as well, and because we are all adults now, giving someone a look is hardly ever wrong. But, I was happy to meet him after a ten-year absence so that we could pick up where we left off. Although I admired the hills' understated beauty, I was unsure if he would miss the conveniences of home.

He.

Dipa was chattering nonstop about life up there as usual on the brief, lovely walk back to the farm. But as I walked behind her, downwind, the evening breeze carrying her heady perfume to my nostrils, I was mesmerized by her mature curves and the glimpses of her silky skin through holes in the saree. So quiet had I become that she had to check behind her a couple of times to make sure I was still following, and I quickly had to glance away lest she think I was looking at her.

She was even more alluring because it was golden hour and the sunlight glistened on her flawless skin. From where I stood, I could see her buttocks swaying as she walked along the path, the hourglass figure between the swell of her bosom and the girth of her hips, the curve of her back, and the blouse open at the back, exposing wide swathes of her firm flesh, held together by a flimsy bow tied at the top, which I was desperately tempted to undo.

She noticed my lack of breath as we crested the hill, which was partly a result of her stunning beauty taking my breath away and partly because I was unaccustomed to activity. I couldn't help but keep staring at her face in an unblinking gaze, making her blush a deeper shade of crimson than even the hues of dusk all about us. The sun was about to set in the mountains that bordered the horizon, and she pointed out her farm down in the valley below.

She grabbed my ear and pulled it, causing me to flinch, and said that I hadn't changed at all and was still just a lamb who followed her about. She had no idea that I was a wolf in sheep's clothing and that my motivations weren't as innocent and innocent as she had thought. She felt she had gone too far after seeing me grimace and knelt down to kiss my ear, which was fairly red. My entire body tingled with joy as her gentle lips caressed my ear and her breasts my arm as the color poured across my face.

CHAPTER 4

She urged that I give her the backpack as well and continue until we reached the farm down below even though it would soon be dark. I was happy for the developing shadows since they covered up a raging boner that was quite out of character for me. I was also eager to go forward because it would give me time to concentrate on other things and calm my hot hormones.

With a bubbling creek winding past it, the cottage with the farmland looked like something out of a picture book. It was even more beautiful than I had pictured it to be. But, these were all insignificant matters in comparison to the significant issue that occasionally surfaced in the front of my jeans.

If it were to be disclosed, it had a mind of its own, was challenging to manage, and would undoubtedly destroy the impression she had built of me since I was a young boy. Even an hour with her would be challenging, let alone a week. I had no notion what to do because I was such a newbie.

She.

He was just as incorrigible as he had been ten years prior, yet he was still adorable. When I moved forward in front of him, I could feel him glancing at me and assessing me with his gaze. Here I was fervently expounding on how much I loved the land, and I could bet that he hadn't understood even a single word. Instead, he would occasionally grunt in difficulty as he navigated the terrain, and his labored breathing would interrupt what was practically a monologue on my part.

We stopped for a break as we neared the top of the hill, which is where I like to take my husband to watch the sunset, because he wasn't used to the exercise and was panting and breathing heavily. I started crying as I remembered the times we had come to witness the sunset but had instead just made out, with him dipping into my valley as the sun vanished into the hills. He reminded me so much of him, not interested in the beauty surrounding, eyes only for me. I noticed that he was looking at me in a similar manner when I grabbed him and, not wanting him to see my tears, I mock-indignantly tugged his ear. He winced, so I instantly knelt down to kiss him and reassure him that I hadn't been too harsh. As my lips caressed his ear, I noticed a blush forming on his gorgeous features.

I noticed a bulge in his groin when he moved back and saw that he had grown in other places as well, so I knew why he had moved back during my welcome hug. As my breasts brushed against his chest and arm, I chastised myself for my indecent thoughts as my breasts began to tingle as well. Before he could object, I took his backpack and sent him on his way, giving him a chance to calm down.

Now that I had the upper hand, I was able to objectify him just as I had done to him earlier. The hunter has changed into the prey. I understood that the dynamics of our connection had altered because Krishna was no longer small and I was no longer his Dipa. He started talking about himself and his life thus far as I pondered

18

all of this in an out-of-the-ordinary stillness, admiring the sight of his virile figure silhouetted against the dusky twilight shadows. It was a new experience for me because I had only occasionally heard him talk, save for the occasional monosyllable.

Although I adored the way his deep, sonorous voice broke the stillness of the evening, my thoughts were elsewhere, just as they had been on the journey up. While licking my lips and examining the succulent piece of prime meat in front of me, I was also imagining possibilities that got me wet again and made me blush at the thought that I could even imagine such a situation. Sure, women can have lustful thoughts as well as passionate and gooey ones; after all, gender equality is a vital human right in the period we live in.

We had already arrived at home before I realized it, and I had become so lost in thought that I had almost stumbled into him. But just as I was about to hit the ground, he grabbed me with his powerful arms. His fingertips stroked my skin, sending a current through me, and I felt his face next to mine. His deep-set eyes looked into mine, wondering if I was alright.

Before looking away and taking a deep breath to calm my racing heart, I came close to kissing him on the lips. I was agitated by my lack of restraint and erred on the verge of acting foolishly. Before things got out of hand, I had to gather myself because if I didn't, he would lose all respect for me and living with him would be torment.

I questioned whether inviting him over was a smart idea because, if things didn't work out, it would ruin the precious childhood memories that meant the world to me. I had just about recovered from an enormous catastrophe when another one threatened to destroy me.

He took an anxious glance at me since I was stuck, absorbed in contemplation, and putting strain on his tendons to keep me off the ground. I steadied myself after sensing his heavy breathing and murmured an apology as I stood up straight. Before we met for dinner below, I showed him to his room, which is adjacent to mine on the first floor, and asked him to change and get ready.

He.

Just about, I had managed to contain the beast that was rearing. Although Dipa was hidden from view behind me in the shadows, she was never far from my thoughts as her alluring aroma filled my nostrils, reminding me of her constant presence and undermining all of my attempts to control my surging hormones. I started talking about myself to divert my attention and to keep the tension low. I surprised both myself and her by my volubility and by her sudden stillness.

When I finally halted at the gate at the bottom of the slope, she unexpectedly bumped into me and staggered, almost sprawling to the ground. My muscles tensed up to keep her upright as I instinctively stretched out and grabbed her before she fell, placing one hand at her back and the other at her waist.

CHAPTER 5

Her face was close to mine, our eyes were locked, and as I lost myself in her depths, her expression changed from one of dread to one of relief. Her lips were barely apart, which sent a stream of sexual energy coursing through me. If I knew how to kiss, I would have given her a quick kiss right then.

She quickly whispered an apology and turned her head away, perhaps saving my face by keeping me from saying something that could have ended our friendship. But I was happy since it gave me a chance to approach her without coming off as rude.

She led me to my room and asked me to freshen myself before we met for dinner. I questioned whether I had a bowel movement because I had traveled far and was sweaty and odorous. I think it's a male thing, but my mother frequently needs to remind me to take a bath since she claims I smell. Just as I was ready to enter the bathroom after changing into a fresh set of clothes, it occurred to me that I had forgotten to inquire about the hot water. The frigid air made me cringe at the prospect, even knowing a cold shower would do much to calm my passion.

To ask her, I went to her room. She was singing in a pleasant voice, and the door was ajar. I took a peek inside, and what I saw left me dumbfounded. She was doing a sensual striptease to the classic song while swaying to the beat with her eyes closed. She appeared even more seductive than Sridevi did in the original version of "I Love You," which goes as follows: "Time slows down with you around, as I can't put what's in my heart to my lips, but I will confess tonight for sure, I Love You."

She twirled around singing slowly unwinding the layers of her saree, bringing the satiny cream petticoat into view. She didn't realize that she had a captive audience, as the door was ajar and her charms were on full view, enhanced by her mellifluous voice and the cool night air, adding to the romance of her uninhibited performance.

My mouth watered at the sight of her soft mounds as I yearned to bury my face in them as she caressed her face with her hands and sucked her fingers suggestively, drawing a sigh from my lips as I watched spellbound. Then she lowered her neck, biting her ruby lips suggestively, parting them to emit a moan as she cupped her breasts through her blouse enhancing her cleavage.

The satiny petticoat sat on her broad hips as she swayed them suggestively from side to side dancing to the beat. There was a slit at the side that teased with glimpses of her pale flesh as she moved lower down to her uncovered tummy with soft rolls of flesh which she stroked making her way to the navel positioned tantalizingly in the center.

She had no bra underneath, and it was my first view of the female breast since I was a baby. She shook her bottom, lifted the hem of the petticoat to her knees, revealing her perfectly formed calves as she twirled around, then put her hand behind her back tugged at the bow releasing it, loosening her blouse.

I wished I was a baby again and could suckle on her breast as her huge jugs came into view, defying gravity, bouncing up and down, palm sized, with a dark pink areola and inverted nipples.

When she opened her eyes and realized that I was standing in the doorway, dreamily staring at her, she screamed and covered her exposed breasts with her hand as I quickly hurried back to my room, slamming the door behind me.

I felt small and worthless, not fit to even look her in the eye, and I wished I had been more discreet and exercised self control, but then I was a novice in such matters. "Shit", I cursed myself, letting forth a volley of unmentionables at my carelessness. I had ruined my reputation forever, what would she be thinking of me, and I felt small and worthless, not fit to even look her in the eye.

She had managed to rouse the beast in me, unearthing feelings that I was surprised to learn existed within me; I resolved not to embarrass her anymore and cut short my trip before I did anything worse and return home at the earliest. Even in college, my friends called me a nerd; I felt no attraction towards the opposite sex; in fact, I tended to avoid them if possible, feeling awkward and tongue-tied with them around.

She.

My bras no longer fit me after becoming pregnant, so even today I was braless under the blouse in the hopes that he wouldn't notice. I was constricted and unaccustomed to wearing a saree, and in fact I loved the freedom that being in such a remote location had provided me, the luxury of not wearing any clothes at all.

My heart was light and aflutter and for some reason I felt sexy again, seen through his eyes, as I slowly shed the layers of clothing that had been covering me. As soon as I got home, I hurried to my room to strip off my clothes and let my skin breathe again. In my haste, I forgot to shut the door because I was not used to company. My luscious flesh was yearning for his touch as I closed my eyes and imagined him stripping off my clothes and caressing me as I performed a seductive striptease just for him. He ran a line of kisses around my navel, which was nestled like a pearl within the soft folds of my undulating stomach, making me groan impatiently. I imagined him reaching behind my back and using his mouth to undo the blouse's knot, revealing my firm

I screamed, instinctively covering my breasts, hoping against hope it was not too late, but I knew instinctively that my meticulously cultivated image from all those years ago was shattered forever. I wish I had been more circumspect as I heard the door to his room slam shut, knowing that nothing that I could say or do would remedy this breach, but so it was.

My loins were wet from my cravings, and a stain had spread to the front of my petticoat, but the recent happenings were like a damp blanket, as the desire faded, replaced with an uneasiness and sorrow. I bolted the door, a little too late, and started to take off the rest of my clothes.

CHAPTER 6

I started the task, hoping it would take my mind off the worst-case scenarios that were constantly running through it because my breasts were hurting from not being milked for so long, and I decided to put on a brave face and accept whatever fate had decreed for me; it was not on purpose, but an accident.

I rummaged through my closet looking for something to put on, but all my nighties were sexy, diaphanous, revealing more than they concealed, more to rouse passions and for my husband to remove, rather than conceal my modesty. I chose the most conservative one of the lot, but I knew I would come off as a vixen having no underwear to wear underneath, but something is always better than nothing.

He was sitting sullenly, eyes downcast, not even giving me a sidelong glance when I went to him, ruffled his hair, and apologized for what had happened earlier, sorry for ruining his holiday. A single tear coursed down my cheek as I said this, as I was really fond of him and was so looking forward to the next fortnight.

I hugged him close as tears of relief spilled out, glad to be on the same page; it was nothing but a misunderstanding, he didn't hate me. But to my surprise, he startled me by gripping me tightly, burying his face in my bosom, and holding back a sob.

My phone buzzed and I saw there were a plethora of missed calls from his home. We realized that he had not called back, and his mom must be frantic by now, organizing a red alert for her missing darling. We laughed together, visualizing it and driving the blues away. He was still sobbing uncontrollably, like a child, so I did what I used to do decades ago, lifted his face and kissed those tears away.

All this melodrama had made me ravenous and I asked him if he was hungry. He replied that he was starving and could eat a horse. So I got busy with the dinner preparations as he set the table. As the aroma of food filled the air, he licked his lips in anticipation, remembering the many meals that I had fed him and was pleasantly surprised that I remembered.

My front was getting wet from sweat and other fluids that were trickling out of a lower orifice, and I sensed his eyes boring into my back in the warm kitchen, realizing that I must be providing the eye candy as an appetizer, with the sweat adding to the translucency of my sheer nightgown. I wished I had put on some pants or a sweater, but grabbed an apron in a last-minute hack to save my modesty the blushes.

I asked him if he would be comfortable with me feeding him, and he was ecstatic at my suggestion. I had cooked his favorite okra, crispy just the way he liked it, a cucumber salad, and his favorite dal fresco. I was flushed from the heat and a little from the excitement, which was more in a couple of hours than the last six months.

My eyes misted over as he brought the food to my mouth; food had never tasted better, and even more so when it was fed with such loving care. Nevertheless, he was not used to feeding me in this manner and spilt quite a bit, causing a mess. However, I was shocked when he insisted on feeding me in return.

He literally licked my fingers clean, saying there was magic in them, making me blush at the compliment. Luckily I had worn the apron, otherwise, I would have to take a bath again. He enjoyed the gajar ka halwa made with carrots grown on the farm itself and said that he wouldn't be able to get through the front door of his own house when he returned.

But I was surprised and a little pleased when he said that there was just one girl he liked and had proposed to her a decade back, but was heartbroken as she had not yet deigned to reply. I was really touched and again misty eyed at his sweet words, he really knew how to make a girl feel good. I also felt a warm fuzzy feeling course through me, and I wasn't sure whether it was good or bad.

I immediately realized that I had made a mistake of judgement as my front was fully drenched in sweat and though he tried his best to avoid looking at me, there was no denying that my charms were out in full view and the wet cloth moulded itself to my skin, exerting a pull that was hard to resist. He offered to help with the dishes and we repaired to the porch to see the stars.

Worse, it was a full moon night, but he had no interest in the stars, but considerably lower down, I could make out the stars in his eyes as he looked at me. I caught him casting a few covert glances towards my boobs and cunt, and only my strategically placed hands, shielded my modesty or what was left of it as I waited for the cool night breeze to dry my clothes.

I tried to show him the constellations in the clear night sky but his interests were firmly rooted in earth. I shivered, feeling the intensity of his passion, wondering where it would take us. I was much more direct in admiring his rippled body dressed in pyjamas and singlet that showed off his muscular arms. At the juncture of his thighs I could discern a growing bulge that confirmed that it was not just sweet talk, but he really meant what he said.

He.

My mind was racing after the debacle that had just happened; I had never felt this way before. After my appalling behavior, I questioned whether I would ever be able to face her again. I made the decision to apologize unconditionally tonight and leave the following morning. Visions of her beauty danced before my eyes, and I couldn't quite understand the sensations that the sight of her brought out in me.

I immediately walked through her closed door to the dining room after changing into my pajamas and singlet. I didn't even dare to look in her direction when I heard her footsteps coming down the stairs in a short while. My thoughts were racing over what she must think of me, likely believing that I am a pervert.

But she approached me, brushed my hair, and said she was sorry. In order to stop me from crying like a child and burying my head in her chest, she lifted my head and kissed my tears away, just like she used to do previously.

CHAPTER 7

My phone had shut off since I had failed to charge it during my stressful moment. In my enthusiasm to see mom again, I entirely forgot about my commitment to phone her as soon as I arrived. However, Dipa and I were back on good terms, so I didn't mind getting scolded by my mother; in fact, I kind of welcomed it after the emotional roller coaster we had just experienced.

After dealing with my mental concerns, I became really hungry because I hadn't eaten well in a while and had been traveling for a few days. For the first time since she descended, I had a clear view of her as she began to make dinner. Her nightgown, which was made of virtually sheer satin, showed off her beautiful body against the light.

My hunger vanished as I drooled at the sight of her slender neck, nearly concealed by her wavy hair that framed her beautiful face, her wide hips, the arch of her back, the breasts protruding from the sides, and her shapely legs leading up to her bouncing buttocks. She radiated beauty from every angle and lacked any undergarments.

I struggled to control my erection as a red-blooded man in my prime and wished I had been wearing underwear to prevent more embarrassment. When I was given a full frontal view, my mind was working overtime as I tried to picture the delight that was in store for me. It like taking a man to an unlimited buffet while he was starving.

I was a little concerned about how I would control my libido while being charmed by her. Nevertheless, she had foreseen this and donned an apron to protect her modesty from my lecherous gaze. I was ecstatic to see that she had prepared all of my favorite foods when dinner was ready. My excitement knew no bounds when she requested if she may feed me with her own hands.

I had never felt such supreme fulfillment, whether it was brought on my my hunger, my favorite foods, or her fingers brushing my lips. I thought I was taking part in naived yam, a sacrifice to God. I tried to feed her in return, but because to my clumsiness, I spilled more than I fed. But, simply the touch of her gentle lips and tongue on my fingers made me feel like I was in heaven.

The pièce de résistance was the gajar halwa, and I was on the verge of licking her fingers completely. We started talking after dinner was finished and the dishes were put away. This time, instead of the prior attempts, which were more of a monologue since I was too preoccupied by her charms to engage in meaningful discourse, we really engaged in dialogue.

She enquired as to whether I had a girlfriend and was very pleased when I replied that I had once proposed to a girl I liked but she had yet to respond. Even though that seemed fairly cliché, it was the truth. The more I viewed her, the more I understood that love at first sight was not at all a myth, and that no girl had ever made me feel the same way before or since.

I questioned whether I could ever be worthy of her love as I watched her, face glowing, arouse desires in me that I never thought existed. We went outside to the porch to watch the sky, but I was only interested in her; the full moon was nothing compared to her allure. She had to take off the apron, which gave me a glimpse of her garden of delights, but she had noticed where my sight was focused and strategically covered it with a hand to block it from my enquiring eyes.

She attempted to pique my interest in the distant stars, but I was firmly fixated on those closer to us. She was glowing from within even though it was pitch black where we were sitting. I could even hear her heartbeat out here because it was so quiet in comparison to the city's clamor.

My attention was firmly fixed on her despite her attempts to persuade me to look away. She eventually grew tired of diverting my focus elsewhere, looked at me, but was unable to meet my piercing glance, and she turned her flushing gaze elsewhere. She reached out for my hand and squeezed it, savoring its firmness in contrast to her own softness.

We sat there, conversing silently but effectively. I immediately wrapped my arm around her as she shuddered and lay her head on my chest. I could smell the fruity scent in her hair and felt moisture on my chest, which led me to believe she was crying once more. Just like she had my tears earlier that evening, I pulled her head up and kissed them away.

The purring cat came over and perched on her lap. Oh I wish I were that fortunate kitty. My eyes began to sag and I struggled to hold back a yawn as I saw her sleeping soundly after the big supper and a hard day were behind me. She got up to walk inside when she noticed me nodding off, but she never let go of my hand. While walking, she retrieved a bottle of water and inquired as to if I needed anything else. She led me to my room, put me to sleep, then got up to leave. But I simply wouldn't release her hand. She sat next to me in bed, kissed me on the forehead, and said, "Good night." I so wanted her to sleep next to me and let me put my hand back up her sleeve, but I lacked the strength or the guts to tell her since I didn't want to hurry things forward and ruin an ideal day. I soon fell asleep quickly.

She.

I lay my head on his chest to get some rest after the evening's excitement and to take a break from using my arms to hide my treasures from his oncoming gaze. My arm grazed his thigh as it descended, and he jerked, drawing my attention to the bulge in his shorts that was tenting.

Tears welled up in my eyes as it brought back bittersweet memories of similar circumstances with my husband. He lifted my cheek to kiss my tears away after detecting them. He held me in his muscular arms, keeping me warm from the brisk breeze while we sat there in silence. He must be tired, I thought, so I heard him yawn and got up to go inside. I led him to his room and tucked him in, but he wouldn't let go of my hand. I then sat next to him, giving him a forehead kiss and telling him good night. He was so exhausted that he fell asleep quickly. I returned to my room after gently prying my fingers out of his hold.

Although I was too excited to sleep, I closed the door. Despite the cold outdoors, I took off my nightgown and sat by the window as the soft moonlight reflected on the river, giving the surroundings and my body within an ethereal dreamy character.

As I replayed the day's events, I noticed a moisture between my thighs and how peaceful the night was. When one hand carelessly played with my nipples and the other caressed the nub of my clitoris, slipping into the folds of my labia, to relieve the itch that wanted attention, my nipples hardened in response to my thoughts. I closed my eyes and let my mind run wild as my thighs spread open to allow free access to my inner depths.

As I got closer to orgasm, my entire body started to move in unison with my thoughts. As my nether regions filled with my love concoctions, my lips parted in a moan. When I said his name aloud, "Krishna," an image of him appeared in my head. And I immediately understood that I loved him in a way that I had earlier refused to admit, and that he had seeped into the corners of my heart.

My thoughts wandered to our final day of contact. On the verge of puberty, my body was going through changes that I couldn't quite understand. A fuzz was starting to appear under my armpits and in my slit, and my breasts were gradually filling up, with small protuberances emerging from what had previously been a flat chest.

When I was bathing him earlier that day, I started to notice that his normally soft pee pee would stand up like a twig when I applied soap to his body. I hadn't previously shown any interest in it, so I quickly finished the bath out of fear that I had done something improper.

Later at night, he reached for my sleeve as usual, but this time, I was wearing a slightly larger kurta to cover up my expanding breasts. He reached a little further than usual, brushing his palms across my breast, which caused it to tense up. I turned to face him and pressed my hips firmly into his, savoring the wonderful sensations. When I held him close to my bosom, I suddenly felt my body trembling and uncontrollable dampness below.

I went to the bathroom to take a closer look because I couldn't figure out what was going on. I could see a wet, sticky substance coming from my slit that was slightly opaque and not at all like my urine. I hadn't noticed it before, but there was a bud near the top that was extremely sensitive to my touch. I tried to push it back in, but every time I did, I felt a rush of pleasure. I soon started rubbing it, first slowly and then more vigorously as I opened out my thighs and let my fingers go to new locations. My body clenched up as I envisioned his hard willy prodding into my depths, and soon a stream of liquid came to the surface. I experienced my first orgasm while self-masturbating, though I was unaware of it at the time.

CHAPTER 8

Following that, I felt a wash of guilt, as if I had done something wrong or humiliating, and I reprimanded myself for having a dirty mind because that was not how a good girl should act. The guilt overtook me and kept me awake the entire night, making it impossible for me to fall asleep. My first period arrived the following morning, and I was scared to see blood oozing from my vagina. Fearing that my time was over and I was going to pass away, I hurried crying to my mother and confessed everything, about what a rotten daughter I had been.

When my mother started to laugh, she grabbed me in her arms, kissed me, and dried my tears. She apologized for not having this conversation with me sooner about birds and bees. I'm grateful to have a parent who is so understanding. She shut the doors and windows, undressed in front of me, and gave me a practical lesson in sex education that I still treasure today.

She continued to explain every aspect in great but useful detail, including sexuality, contraception, periods, masturbation, and hygiene as I watched on in astonishment and admiration of her forthrightness and sagacity as I stared wide-eyed at her mature body, large breasts, puffy mound, and wide hips. She broke down every aspect of the human anatomy for me and even showed me how to enjoy oneself, dispelling the notion that doing so was wrong or filthy.

She carefully responded to all of my inquiries and helped me feel at ease with my sexuality. I gave her a hug after she was done, grinning as she kissed me and gave me a sanitary napkin to wear while she showed me how to use it. I slept next to her for the following few nights until we had to part ways.

Regrettably, my dad was relocated up north, and I became preoccupied with my studies and never returned to my hometown village. Even after all these years, I can still clearly recall that day, and when I look in the mirror, I'm struck by how much my mother looks like me. I aspire to be as independent, liberal, and forward-thinking as my mother, who raised us all. After tidying up, I went to bed, cuddling my pillow and drifting off to sleep with memories of the three people I loved most in the world: my mother, my husband, and my Krishna.

He.

I awoke from a deep sleep to the sweetest tune resonating in my ears. It took me a while to remember where I was and that I had "morning wood," as it was called. She was singing in her singsong way and watering the plants when I opened the window to let some fresh air in, which was a beautiful sight to behold. I was transfixed as she appeared to be an angel engulfed in the early mist, with a voice to match, and I suspected that I would have trouble controlling the rising.

She waved to me as she noticed me standing at the window. She beckoned me down as I fell to my knees and offered me her most brilliant smile. I changed out of my pajamas and put on a fresh pair of underwear before going to the bathroom to brush my teeth and get ready. It was a wonderful beginning to a new day, and I was determined to get off to a good start and leave a good impression on her because I couldn't stop thinking about her.

I came downstairs with my coat in hand and stopped at the kitchen refrigerator to get a bottle of milk, which I drank to bolster myself. I drank the entire bottle because it was the sweetest, tastiest milk I had ever tasted. It was so different from the packaged milk you get in the city.

She captivated me as I entered the yard because, in the early morning light, she appeared even more stunning. She asked how I was sleeping and apologized for waking me up with her singing, but I said that I wouldn't mind staying up all night to hear her wonderful voice. She mock-punched me and declared that I was a real lady killer with both my words and appearance, and that she envied the girl who would succeed in bagging me.

If only she knew that I had already discovered my dream girl and didn't need to look any further, I would not have blushed at her compliments. She asked me whether I was up for a yoga session and said that if not, she would do it after making the breakfast. I informed her that I previously had a bottle of the most delectable milk from her refrigerator and noted that, in contrast to the milk at home, it definitely must have come from happy cows.

When it was her turn, she blushed, which complemented her lovely features and looked good on her. She unzipped two mats, lay them out on the lawn, took off her coat, and started the lesson. The same nightgown that she had worn the night before was still on, and in the sun, more of her was visible than in the dark.

Her breasts were stunning, and I instantly focused on them to get a close-up look at her assets after accidentally spotting them from a distance last night. I was a little saddened to see that she was wearing underwear that covered her loins when my sight dipped lower past her belly button. But despite being covered in lace and ribbons that revealed hints of the soft flesh inside, they were the sexiest pair of underwear I had ever seen.

Although I was relieved to be wearing underwear, my erection was starting to feel very uncomfortable. As she saw that I was ogling her big possessions, she told me to stop and pay attention. She put her body through a number of poses over the course of the next half-hour, making it difficult for even an athlete like myself to keep up. I was in awe of her flexibility and grace from every aspect, and by the time we were finished, I was panting and saturated.

I occasionally caught her peeking at me, but not with my piercing glance, which literally stripped her with my eyes. By the time we were finished, she gave me a hug and complimented my toned and well-maintained figure while telling me that I had done a wonderful job despite having to adjust to the rarefied mountain air.

But I dismissed it, saying that she usually applied a lot of butter and that with a teacher as talented as she was, even a moron like me would undoubtedly advance.

CHAPTER 9

She praised me for my repartee and said she appreciated it, but she said she preferred the little lamb I had been the night before, not the big evil wolf I had become.

I pretended to be hurt by her words, and she came over to ruffle my hair and apologize. However, I couldn't help but smile, and she realized that it was a ruse to win her sympathy. She then stuck her tongue out at me and said that she meant every word she said, and we both burst out laughing until our sides hurt, falling into each other's arms for support.

I enjoyed cradling her in my arms once more and felt her warm, soft body against mine. She also realized it, so she took a step back, put her coat on, and entered the house to make breakfast. I hung around like a lovesick puppy as I watched her potter about the kitchen as she went about her work, completely enamored by her numerous talents.

I said that anything would be great as long as she fed me when she asked what I wanted for breakfast. She said that I would be completely spoiled by the time I returned, and that my mother had warned her cousin about this happening because she knew how much she loved me. She told me that I had to help out around the house since I was no longer a little child who required constant feeding and because there was no such thing as a free meal.

I had been enjoying seeing her from behind up until this point, so I was delighted to have a closer look at her features and enjoy breathing in her aroma, which was mingled with the seductive sweat she had produced after the workout. She instructed me to prepare the mushrooms and carrots while she made the Dalia, adding sauteed mushrooms, baby carrots, and fresh herbs from the garden as a side dish.

I was accustomed to living in dorms while in college, so I was familiar with kitchen duties. In addition, my mother had given me good training. She claimed that my wife would be overjoyed to have a prized catch trained to assist with chores like me. She intended to tease me and pull my leg, but I didn't bat an eye and just responded I know as I gazed into her beautiful eyes.

I spoke with complete sincerity, and she once more reddened as her focus briefly wandered and she burned her finger on the splattering oil. She pulled my hand away out of habit, but I held it and sucked on her fingers until she felt better because she preferred to avoid looking into my eyes. As I was finishing the food, I seated her at the table.

I insisted on giving her breakfast, telling her that it would allow her to evaluate the beta version's improvements and determine for herself how different I had become. She agreed but explained that because of the injury to her right hand, she would be unable to feed me. Although I was fast to react, I understood that she was merely playing me again. I wouldn't eat if she didn't feed me with her left, though.

She was baffled and thought I was insane, but she sniffed into her sleeve because I had touched her. She enjoyed the sensation of her soft lips enclosing my fingers as I fed her, getting a little better with repetition. She said that she could adjust to this way of life, but as I pointed out, the tables had now turned.

She deliberately bit my fingers, and when I pulled them away while pretending to be in pain, she grabbed my hand to examine the harm she had done. She refused to eat any more food when I laughed and told her I was joking, stating it was pointless to laugh about since she had almost missed a heartbeat. With due remorse, I offered my apology. Another of her hilarious regulations struck me at this point: we didn't need to stand on protocol, so please don't say sorry or thank you.

She insisted on giving me breakfast with her right hand, keeping her injured pinky at a distance. I told her it was great and she agreed, but she insisted that since I had taken the time to prepare it, I should get the credit. After breakfast, she showed me how to utilize the warm water and get ready quickly because she wanted to show me about the farm.

She.

I dreamed of him and a pillow between my legs when I woke up in the morning, with a moist spot growing where my thighs met. My breasts were sensitive, so I milked them to lessen the fullness I felt. After that, I relieved the itch lower down by closing my eyes and pressing the buttons that released the flow of desire to empty out my slit.

As I opened the windows to let the cool morning breeze in, the sun's earliest rays were peeking out from behind the hills, giving my exposed skin goosebumps. I pulled on my nightgown and searched the cabinet for any underwear to hide my privates from his view, but all I could find was seductive lingerie. I settled on a lacy white undershirt because it was better than nothing. I also grabbed a coat to keep me warm and shield my chest from the morning breeze.

When I was exploring the flora in the garden, a surge of joy swept over me, causing me to start singing. I took the hose and started watering the shrubs when I suddenly looked up to saw him at the window staring at me intently as if trying to make up for the decade he had missed. I returned his smile and invited him to come outside and sit with me in the garden.

After a time, he returned, looking quite revived but also a little dejected that the free performance I had given him the previous evening had come to an end. The relaxation and the familiarity helped him to liberate his tongue from its restraints, and as a result, the conversation was sharp and the humor was crackling. Despite the fact that his legs were long enough, I seized every opportunity to pull them, but he gave as good as he got in return.

When I asked him if he could wait for breakfast, he said that he wasn't in a rush because he had already consumed the entire bottle of milk. When I realized that the milk he had enjoyed so much was the one I had expressed just an hour before, I blushed. Yet, I didn't want to further humiliate him by revealing this information; I would rather keep some things a secret.

He joined me as I began a series of yoga poses and warm-ups. But, I could feel parts of me clenching rather than loosening since he was concentrating more on my body than his own. He started to sweat while attempting to keep up with me, and I began to question whether it was such a good idea after all. As we went inside for breakfast, I took my time, saying a few encouraging words to keep him from getting discouraged. As we laughed, the discomfort of the previous evening vanished into a comfortable camaraderie.

I asked him for assistance as I made breakfast because I was uncomfortable with his unwavering focus and asked him to give me some eye candy as well. While he assisted in chopping the veggies, I caught a breath of his masculine aroma and told him that he would be a prize catch and his wife would be over the moon.

He then flipped my comment back on me, which made me look away from the burner and caused some hot oil to sputter on my finger. Yet, he appeared to be completely charmed with me. He slipped my finger into his mouth to cool it off as I reflexively drew it out, but as he did so, a sense of warmth crept throughout my body, resulting in a flush on my cheeks and a dampness infiltrating my lower lips.

Despite the fact that he insisted on feeding me and had significantly improved since yesterday night's mishap, I mock-bited him to demonstrate how it would be like putting his hand in a lioness' mouth. He feigned pain as he winced, but I was irritated with him for abusing my concern and reminded him that it wasn't a joke.

CHAPTER 10

After this reprimand, he was suitably sorry and feeling a little defeated, but he resisted eating until I gave in and fed him with my own hands.

I could see that he was deeply in love with me as well, and I was madly in love with him with every passing second, but I wasn't sure if our relationship would last. I made a decision to put some distance between us, stop the runaway wagon, and allow us some time to consider it.

We had to get ready because we were going on a farm tour. As he had already seen a lot of mine, I invited him to go up ahead so I could see his cute butt. I demonstrated how to operate the geyser to him before returning to mine to start the bath and take a soothing dip. I started to hum a song from an old Hindi movie as the tub filled with water and steam ascended.

I sang, "Bhai batur, bhai batur, Ab jayenge kitni door, Nazuk nazuk meri jawaani, Chalne se majboor," while filling the bathtub. Roughly translated, this song means "dear friend, I have reached adulthood; it is up to us how far we go together in this voyage of love."

As I undressed and slid into the warm water, I closed my eyes and visualized his virility naked in the shower. I then let my fingers play out my fantasies once more as the humming gave way to a series of moans, as my pleasure points once more became activated, and as waves of gratification swept over me.

The response "Yeah Dipa" and the first notes of another song, roughly translated as "You should always have a bath with cold water, even if you don't know how to sing, you will burst into song," came from the opposite side. I discovered too late that the bathrooms shared a single wall and that the vents to let the steam out were connected, allowing the sound to pass through plainly as well. I reddened the entire length of my torso as a result.

All of my carefully considered attempts to create some distance between us failed after a short period of time as I worried about how to salvage the circumstance. I wondered if he found my groans to be hard or if he found them repulsive and scandalous since they were so overtly sexual. I made the decision to exercise restraint over bravery in the hopes that he wouldn't bring up the subject once more if I let sleeping dogs lie.

I hurriedly finished the remainder of my bath in silence and changed into a loose-fitting shirt, some denim shorts, and one of his Stetson hats to complete the appearance. The shorts were certainly too tight when I looked in the mirror because I hadn't taken into consideration my postpartum changes, but the shirt effectively covered my breasts. I let the shirt hang loose, allowing it fall over my hips as well, and I went downstairs to wait for him. He arrived downstairs looking sharp in a singlet that highlighted his toned arms and rippling biceps and a matching pair of denim shorts. As he noticed me, he gave a low whistle, and I blushed once more, turning my head away. He asked me why I had stopped singing as he descended because he was eager to play antakshari with me because I had such a good voice. He questioned whether the end of the song's sensual chorus of aahs was actually there or if I had made it up on my own.

I pretended to punch him in anger to try to cover up my shame because I knew he had me by surprise. Yet, it released the tension in the room, and the talk resumed its normal flow. We took a stroll around the farm, which covered the entire valley; the closest neighbors were at least 20 miles distant. When I first saw it, I shrieked with joy at having a bit of heaven just outside my door. I couldn't bear the thought of ever returning to the city, which now seemed so foreign to me, or living anywhere other than this slice of paradise.

I wanted him to notice it the same way I did, but he was staring at me as usual. He was completely beyond saving, yet he was also fairly innocent and ignorant of worldly issues. When we got to the stream, the water was knee-high, so we had to ford it. We took off our boots and slung them around our necks as we sat down. While I was finishing, I noticed that he was staring at my legs, but at that point, I was also acting like a high school girl in love.

Just as I was about to warn him to use caution when crossing the gap, he lost his feet and fell heavily on me as I stumbled to maintain my position. I instructed him to continue walking forward while keeping an eye on the road in the hopes of escaping his steadfast attention. In reality, I like the attention he gave me, albeit sometimes it was a bit excessive and gave him time to reflect as well. But he had a better idea, so I had to abandon my plan to create some distance between us. Instead, we could walk together.

We had to keep close because the road was tight, which suited him well because his arm constantly touched the side of my breast, electrifying me from head to toe. Not that I objected, but it was a precipice that might lead us in an unexpected direction. He opened the front of his vest as the sun was rising, and I drooled when I saw his gleaming abs and six pack. I also unfastened a few buttons and caught him trying to look down my cleavage a few times. I was relieved that it was loose enough not to expose my nipples, which were now really aroused.

He was uninterested in my attempts to describe the variety of flora that covered the land. He asked me to feed him and him when we stopped to pick some berries. We grabbed a few apples, oranges, and mangoes that were just beginning to mature. I folded the bottom of my shirt and tied them up, showing his curious gaze my tight shorts and a small portion of my stomach.

Then, as I watched in dread, he slid, a disaster waiting to happen, tumbling right into the nettle-filled bramble bushes. As he winced in pain from the nettles' stings, I sprinted after him without caring about the fruits that had fallen out. I looked into his eyes, relieved that they were unharmed, and then I despised myself for allowing it to happen as I started to cry.

He was now covered in a red rash and swollen from agony as I held his head in my lap and carefully tried to remove the bunches that were still clinging to his skin.

CHAPTER 11

His body was now covered with the rash, and he was on the verge of writing from the inability to remain still. I froze, worry written all over my face, clutching him to my chest, trying to figure out what to do.

I started to kiss him to soothe the pain, but as I did, the nettle sting lodged on my lips, making them swell. We were both now in the same situation, although I just had localized discomfort that was most severe where my skin was most sensitive. In hindsight, that was a poor decision. Thoughts of suffering, though, rekindled a connection that had been dormant in my childhood memory bank. I recalled a trip to the village of our ancestors, where a young child had also discovered these very bushes. As his mother applied her milk to the rashes as instructed by the wise old woman, he quickly recovered. I made the decision to try it, turned away from him, unfastened my shirt's buttons, and attempted to express my milk to ease his suffering.

Nevertheless, my usually full breasts—which were always soft and full—had dried up in some way, and no amount of stroking them produced even a single drop of my elixir. As the minutes passed, I became increasingly helpless and stressed out about how to initiate the flow. I made the decision to gamble.

I faced him with my torso exposed as he turned to stare at them once more in shock, staring at my rack for the second time in less than a day, this time not by accident, and wondering what the heck I was up to. I placed one on his lips and invited him to suckle. He was conflicted and in pain, but he had a hard time comprehending the wonderful fortune that was right in front of him. As a result, he didn't need a second invitation to latch on like a helpless infant. When the trigger came, my mammaries immediately began to flow once more. When I applied milk to his torso, he switched from one boob to the other, milk running down his face as the rashes began to magically vanish. I was ecstatic to see him no longer in pain, but I was also dumbfounded since my lips had grown very large and tears of ecstasy were flowing down my face. As my tears saturated his hair, he turned to face me. His relief quickly turned to concern when he observed my swollen lips, and he brought his lips close to mine, the milk covering them doing wonders to lessen the swelling and restore the sensations. Yet neither he nor I stopped because we had passed the Rubicon; our friendship had moved beyond the platonic to something much deeper than it had ever been.

He.

I half expected her to give me a bath like she had done when she showed me how to start the hot water, but I was an adult now, so she left me alone with my thoughts. I took off my clothes, but it was still difficult as my mind sought to remember my younger years. Much more so if she had been naked, I would have loved to have had her bathe me, but it would be challenging to control that protruding organ.

I started to massage it carelessly while I savored the warm shower's spray, and I could hear a tinny humming coming from the opposite side. I turned off the shower so I could focus while seeing her singing while she washed herself. She yelled my name aloud as she ran out of things to say and finished in a succession of sexy aahs.

Being a bathroom singer myself, I assumed she wanted to hear me sing and gave her a song of my own in return. I assumed I was singing out of tune and she couldn't stand the torment any longer, but all I got in response was a perplexing stillness. After taking a bath, I changed into a singlet and pair of denim shorts and descended the stairs.

She was waiting for me looking lovely in a blouse a few sizes too big almost fully covering a pair of teensy denim shorts that felt like they had been painted on, a Stetson to finish the look, and tiny denim booties to complete the look. As I made my way down the steps, I couldn't help but whistle softly as I noticed this ghost. I urged her to resume singing in the hopes that I wasn't singing off pitch, but she gave me a mocking punch instead.

Even though it was a gorgeous day, I found it impossible to look away from her slender legs, especially when we paused to take our boots off before crossing the creek. I almost tipped her and I into the chilly water despite her warnings to be careful and watch my step.

But as I was being held in those gentle arms, she caught me just in time, and I received a breath of her divine scent. Although my legs were numb, I felt as though all of my blood had gone to another limb that was pressing up against my shorts. She asked me to walk ahead, but I opted to walk alongside her and enjoy the sensation of my arm brushing against her breast as we traveled along the crowded sidewalk.

She offered me some of the nicest berries I had ever tasted as we were stopping to gather fruit, which were made much sweeter by her own sweet scent. I opened my singlet as the weather warmed up and noticed that she was making passionate eye contact with my abs, which I had worked on to get in shape. I attempted to peak at her cleavage while she undid a few buttons on her shirt, but she caught me and I had to give up.

She gathered some fruit in the bottom of her blouse as we advanced, showing off her shorts and a bit of her midriff. I lost my balance as the loose dirt crumbled beneath my foot, sending me sliding into the brambles, as we were on a little elevated section of the trail as it curved uphill.

She ran after me only to discover that I was covered in nettles, which gave me a rash and was both painful and uncomfortable. She removed all of the nettles, but I was still writhing in agony from the rash, which was causing me a great deal of suffering. She chastised herself for not taking better care because it was torturous for her to watch me writhe like this. She attempted to kiss away my suffering, but it was unsuccessful.

She made a U-turn as she searched for a solution. When she came back to face me, I was left with no choice but to watch in rapt fascination as she unbuttoned her shirt, exposing once more my ample rack, but this time it was no accident.

CHAPTER 12

She approached me and extended her breast to me. Without questioning, I did what she said and started to suck greedily as her milk came out quicker than I could take it in.

I switched back and forth between the breasts, the redness on my face getting better as the milk ran over it. All of the discomfort was instantly relieved once she applied it like a salve. I looked up anticipating rain as I felt my hair getting wet. Yet all I could make out were her streaming tears and her lips swelling shut in pain from the nettles.

When I put my lips next to hers, the milk contained therein quickly reduced the swelling. That was my first time locking lips, and it felt so fantastic that neither she nor I wanted to quit. My hands reached out to stroke her breasts, feeling their softness between my fingers, and pinching the nipples until they stood up like nubs. Her tongue was pursuing mine and grappling with it as her hands were at the back of my head, holding it there should I move it.

We fled panting, not recognizing when a medical treatment had changed into passion and that nothing would ever be the same again. It had saved both of our lives. She sighed and threw her head back as she cared for me with her generous milk supply since I couldn't get enough of it.

When I realized that I had been enjoying her milk that morning, the riddle of her blushing when I informed her I had never tasted such sweet milk before was resolved. Even though her breasts were now dry, a wet spot was developing in the exact same spot on both her and my shorts. We awoke exhausted but with enough vigor to make the trip home.

She didn't wear a shirt since even the delicate fabric appeared to chafe her breasts, which were too tender and red from my eager sucking. As we stumbled back home, she gathered the fruits in her shirt and slung it over her shoulder, her firm breasts standing tall like an Amazon and defying gravity by offering us an arm.

She doused me in the stream on the way back, suggesting it would lessen the itchiness that was still present, even though the chilly water knocked the wind out of me. Not wanting to miss out on the fun myself, I splashed her back, which made her dripping furious. We quickly grabbed towels from the line, wrapped them around our waists, and removed our damp shorts as we made our way inside the home, shivering in the midday sun.

After an exciting and adventurous morning, we felt comfortable in our own skin as we sat at the kitchen table while she started a tureen of steaming soup to boil. We were becoming more at ease walking around the home bare-chested when I saw that her elevated nipples had fallen flush with the rest of her bosom. She noticed how amazed I was and asked me what I was so bewildered about.

I was honest with her about my feelings, admitting that I knew nothing about the fairer sex and that I was a complete newbie in these issues. During lunch, she offered to take a class on sex 101, and I enjoyed how open she was about her feelings for passion. I offered right away to enroll in the course because I knew I wouldn't find a teacher as good as her anywhere else and I was extremely excited to learn from her.

She offered me a taste of what was to come, claiming that intercourse happened between the ears rather than the thighs. She instructed me to simply look at her breasts, and the nipples protruded to points from the surface without a single touch. She told me that while she could teach me everything about making love, she wasn't interested in fucking because there was a difference between the two.

She promised to teach me everything she knew, and by the time my vacation was through, I would have a Degree in these subjects and would find it difficult to fight off advances from the fairer sex. She chuckled when I told her that I was a one-woman man. She found that life has many unexpected turns and that one should constantly be open to new experiences, take each day as it comes, and never rule anything out.

According to her, treating your spouse with respect and understanding when to draw the line with a firm "no" was the first step. Sexuality shouldn't be suppressed and, as her mother had taught her, is one of the most beautiful forms of expression that is uniquely human.

Five love lessons.

She.

We transformed every equation between us with just one kiss, unleashing a torrent of passion in the process. For a newbie who avoided speaking to women altogether, he had a respectable technique and picked up the job's intricacies quickly. He was attentive to my every need, instantly making adjustments as necessary, reading my emotion before I could ever speak, and carrying out all of my requests as though they were orders.

He drained me dry because he couldn't get enough of me; all that was left was for me to burp him. I didn't even bother putting on my shirt because the sun and breeze would eventually dry out my fragile breasts, which were already sore from his manipulations. In addition, he had experienced them through touch, taste, and sight, so I had no obligation to play coy. While I worked alone, I typically didn't wear a stitch, which was OK with me because I felt good about myself.

The thrill was too much for the day, even though we hadn't even made it halfway around the farm. In addition, he was hobbling and in need of my support after fracturing his ankle on the way down, and needed my support. Therefore, we turned around and headed back toward the creek. I dove him into the freezing overflow from the snow melt that fed the stream since I had read that cold water is a good remedy for nettle stings.

He gasped in response to the cold, losing all sense of breath, yet doused me in good fun. The delicate love he had just experienced lifted his spirits, and he dragged me down onto him until I was very soaked and spluttering in frustration. He made a strong case while touching my lips and remarked that I too had nettle stings.

A cool wind came over as we emerged wet, giving me chills and sending us shivering back into the cozy warmth of the house.

CHAPTER 13

We used the bath towels that were drying on the line to dry off and change out of our wet shorts before heading into the kitchen.

While we waited for lunch to be done, I set a tureen of broth on the burner and we sat down at the table to eat some fruit. He was once more gazing at me and appeared a little bewildered. He inquired as to the whereabouts of my missing nipples. But, just thinking about them caused them to spring up once more from the surrounding breast.

Now that I had four mangoes, I took the ones we had earlier harvested and put them near to my breasts. I questioned him about the abundance of mangoes we gorged on every summer in the hamlet, gorging on them voraciously. The same applied to the breasts; you began with a little touch, worked to prepare them, and then sucked the moisture out of them. I practiced the technique on a mango before clumsily devouring it, the liquid dripping down my neck and down my chest.

I invited him to try it as I hung my lovely fruits in front of him, licking my lips with their tart taste. He tentatively kissed me on the lips first, then trailed down to the boob, alternating it with the mango, as I reclined on the table to sip my mango milkshake. He licked me dry, and I just let my head fall back and relished the sensation. As I teased his nipples with my fingers till they were sharp as well, albeit not as obvious as mine, I asked whether he was satisfied with my nipples at this point.

I admired his innocent simplicity and asked, without waiting for an answer, if he would be interested in some sex education after lunch. He excitedly nodded. The soup was ready, and when combined with some freshly made garlic toast that he helped me make, it gave us both the nourishment we needed and the internal warmth we both so needed to match the warmth of our affections for one another. We obviously fed each other, but he was eager to finish because my offer had aroused both his curiosity and arousal. After lunch, with the kitchen spotless, we retired to the cozy confines of the lounge where I started my master lesson. First, I outlined the ground rules, saying that my comfort and his were equally important. If at any point, either of us felt uncomfortable, we could simply lift our hands and withdraw. It would take the form of a truth-or-dare game that was played with the intention of learning more and becoming more at ease with our bodies and one another rather than for cheap thrills. Until we became weary or ran out of time, the questions would bounce back and forth from one to the other.

I began by inquiring about his range of sexual knowledge and/or experience. He was taken aback by my candor, but said that his only exposure to sex education at school didn't amount to much. He also claimed that he could never comprehend girls or find any of them attractive, which is why the events of the previous day likely exceeded the entirety of his life combined. His thirst for more was only increased by the fact that he had not only seen but also tasted his first breast since infancy, as well as recently had his first liplock.

It was now his turn, and he made the rather timid dare: Could I teach him how to kiss? Well, I could, and I could do it with a method that would make a serial kisser blush. I would give him a variety of exhausting kisses to practice. I began with an insincere "air kiss," which was really more of a peck on the cheek. He argued that I had taken his statements out of context and that this was not what he had meant. He turned away with a nasty expression.

He warmed back up to me, and I gave him my first lip lock, followed by a French kiss, showing the delicacy of a technique we had tried earlier that morning. He finished with a hickey on the neck to remember me by. I offered myself as a volunteer to help him hone his technique and informed him that while he was decent for a novice, he would need to practice to be flawless. The most important thing to remember is that it shouldn't be pushed and should instead flow, providing equal enjoyment for both partners. He didn't mind further demonstrations, but there wouldn't be much time left for anything else, and before he could graduate from my institution, we had to finish the entire curriculum. He still had a lot of work to do to become a master of sex.

It was now my time, so I asked him if he had ever taken himself in hand after noticing his pecker poking out from between the folds of his towel. He blushed when I asked him directly whether he had masturbated because he was such a sweetheart and didn't understand what I was alluding to. He swiftly answered "no," which caused me to raise an inquisitive eyebrow. He then, feeling embarrassed, said that he had occasionally woken up wet and sticky after a very sexual dream, most recently this morning, but felt regret that followed him for days.

My mother's advice from years ago, that giving in to your urges was not a sin but the most natural thing in the world and made the world a safer place to be in, rang true in my years, and I repeated it word for word. When I promised to teach him some methods for future use whenever he felt the need to be excessively urgent, he enthusiastically accepted the offer.

I also had a stake in the outcome because I hadn't seen a live specimen in six months and hadn't bathed him in more than ten. I pulled on the towel that was tucked under his shirt as he looked away, ashamed to be seen in his birthday suit. As the towel came loose, his very impressive specimen almost swatted my breasts.

I stared at it with wide-open eyes, enjoying its length and bulk. Although I hadn't personally seen many outstanding examples of manhood—just my spouse and this man—it was true that he was one of the best. Its size was fairly impressive for one that was in excellent condition and had scarcely been used, yet it seemed to be the ideal size for my receptacle and would fit my socket perfectly. I drooled at the idea, and a glob of saliva landed on the mushroom cap.

CHAPTER 14

I kept myself busy by examining his items. The weeds needed to be trimmed because there were pests in the jungles below, but other than that, it was in excellent condition and twitched as my fingers caressed its length and juggled the balls in the sac below. I checked the box for size, but it was actually only incidental. The functional test for virility was more crucial.

I was anticipating it like I was going for a test drive in a new car, licking my lips as I turned the shifter. A little bead that glistened like a jewel as my fingers massaged his length as he closed his eyes and moaned was a sign of good things to come. He felt some discomfort as the fiction accelerated as I picked up the pace. He had never heard of a tit fuck, but it seemed interesting, so I asked if he was up for one.

I knelt down on the ground between his knees, put his prick between my breasts, expressed some milk to make them slippery, and then jerked him off. I took him to paradise by squeezing his tip into my mouth, looking into his eyes while giving him a blow job he would never forget, and letting him spurt generous reserves of his cream into the moist confines of my mouth as ropes of his baby batter filled me up to the point where I had to swallow to make room for more. As the pace quickened and he pulsated with anticipation.

It was good to taste concentrated man protein once more, and I enjoyed the flavor's strong, smoky aftertaste, greedily consuming it without losing any of his seed. He laid back, fatigued but content, fully blown, in another realm entirely. In the meantime, I was having just as much fun, dripping copiously onto the towel, which nearly came undone from my efforts. I finished the task by slipping a finger into my folds, moaning softly as I cleaned myself out, picturing his plug in my socket.

He ruffled my hair as I had done for him numerous times as he slowly regained his strength, stating that he regretted waiting so long to do it and that if he had known it would be a part of his daily routine, he would have done it morning, noon, and night. Afterwards, still feeling humiliated, he asked me if girls also did it.

I grinned and informed him that we weren't dubbed the fairer sex for nothing since we could experience several orgasms, whilst males could only have one and needed time to recover before experiencing another. I admitted to him that I always had a string of them before night and as soon as I woke up in the morning. When he had recovered his breath, I slyly informed him that I had only fingered myself, and he appeared unable to believe me.

Then, I did something I hadn't planned to do: I stood up and gave him a taste of myself by kissing him. "Shit, I missed the main show," he said after turning back and noticing the wet patch on the towel. He moistened his fingers with my essence and tasted my juice, entering into a trance as he closed his eyes and savored my sweetness.

I advised him not to stress out too much. A full fortnight of opportunities lay ahead of us. Then I said softly in his ear that I had called out his name as I approached and that the oohs and aahs he had heard at the conclusion of my morning performance were the consequence of me flicking my clit in the bathtub. So when he questioned me about it in the morning, I flushed. It simply piqued his curiosity about learning more, but I didn't want to overwhelm him with information and instead chose to dispense it in manageable chunks. I advised him to occasionally take control of himself rather than stifle his urges.

He asked me to describe the various erogenous zones and how to stimulate them when it was his time. I noted that there were plenty, but that if you focused on just one, the others wouldn't matter. He turned to look at my groin, but I gave him a light smack and told him that I hadn't anticipated him to be so narrow-minded and that he needed to focus on cleaning out his head of the dirt that had gathered over the years. He didn't comprehend when I pointed at my head because he was a little slow to get on. He eventually realized that it was all in the mind and that it was, in fact, located in the region between the ears.

I continued by giving a concrete example of the same, pointing out that while both sexes shared some characteristics, they also possessed those that were specific to their sex. It didn't really matter whether I started from the bottom up or the tip to the toe, so I stopped debating. He vigorously nodded in agreement when I added that, especially when you're over over heels in love, the entire body very much functions as an erogenous zone.

CHAPTER 15

As I started the instruction, I asked him to imitate my actions. He ran his hand through my hair after I fluffed up his. I then started to work my magic on him, feeling his pulse speed as I nibbled on his earlobe and licked the back of his ear. He was a quick learner and added a touch of his own, by sucking on them, while I sighed with pleasure.

Next were the lips, which had the most nerve endings and were one of the most sensitive areas of the body, and he began to excite mine as much as I did his, stuck together, as if a vacuum held us together. Up next was his neck, and I taught him to construct a hickey, using his teeth and deep suction to leave a mark that stuck out, as I pushed my neck back whining, as he did the joy of branding me.

I asked him if he would like to perform the honours in my underarms, as his were a touch too hairy for my comfort. I raised up my silky armpits, releasing my pheromones as he took in a long whiff, closed his eyes as he inhaled. He then licked them with gusto, tasting my peculiar flavor, prompting my sluice gates lower down to overflow.

I then dragged my nails on the inner folds of his elbow, while he writhed in excitement and he didn't miss a trick. I then extended my palm to his lips and let him explore it on his own, before putting my slender fingers inside his lips requesting him to suck them as I did his, triggering fellatio on his as he groaned in delight.

I used these very same fingers to follow the length of his spine making him shudder in anticipation as I reached his butt and pinched his taut buns, driving my nails into his sacral dimples. Meanwhile, he relished my curve of my spine and the smooth bounce of mine, trying to enter his hands under the waistband of the towel, before I stopped him, knowing fully well that I wouldn't be able to control myself once he breached there.

I now sucked his cute little nipples, flicking them with my tongue and grazing them with my teeth as his midgets strove to resemble my mature boobs. He didn't need much of an invitation as he latched on to my, enjoying a milkshake from his own cow, as I fed him with my affection. I directed him to the valley of my cleavage and the underside, so as not to miss even one inch of my ripening mounds, as I flung my head back and moaned in delight.

I then moved to his navel, tracing my tongue around it, before zeroing out on the middle. He loved the silky folds of my skin, as I undulated my stomach, guiding his tongue to the soft folds of my belly button, that mirrored a deeper imprint a scant six inches lower, beyond his sight and reach. He had reached as far as he could advance, since I was not yet ready to disclose my crown jewels to his eager gaze.

Now I bowed down in all humility, he was standing stiff at attention, while I began to perform the honours. First I pushed my fingers into his perineum, circled his asshole before inserting a well greased digit to explore unexplored area, while enclosing his ball sac in my pliant lips, as he caressed my hair. I then progressed up his shaft, paying particular attention to his frenulum, making him dance to my rhythm. I rimmed his sensitive glans with my teeth, before swallowing him completely.

He thrust upwards, groaning as my tongue snaked around him, coaxing his cream out of him, milking him dry as he screamed my name out loud as he shivered into my mouth. My vulva responded with an encore as my fingers flicked my clitoris in the towel's folds beneath the hood.

He was panting from the pleasure, so I scooped out a small amount of my cream and tasted it myself before giving it to him. I did this to revive him and thank him for being such a wonderful boy. He greedily drank the moisture from my fingers and demanded more; I gave in because I had plenty to spare.

Then, when he groaned because he hadn't yet replenished his energy and was still softly plopping down next to my cheek, I licked his inner thighs. I questioned him about whether he was through for the day or up for more, but he was a stickler for punishment. Who wouldn't be, given that receiving punishment is so enjoyable that it practically tempts you to commit sex crimes? I was surprised despite my experience and intelligence because I should have seen them coming and expected this would happen. He then looked into my eyes and uttered the dreaded three words, "I love you," followed by the four words, "will you marry me," that were just as fresh today as they were when he had said them more than ten years earlier.

And even more naively, I couldn't help but say, "I love you too," sealing the deal and closing any possible exits. I corrected myself for the hastily spoken remarks, only to later regret them. He was undoubtedly thinking with his dick about love and other things, and I had also let passion to cloud my judgment.

He looked at me beaming like he was the happiest man in the world as I came out with a rider to try to salvage the situation as well as I could. You know nothing of love, yet in less than a day of meeting me, after a decade apart, have proposed marriage. I will not grace you with a reply right away, though my entire being resonates with your love, and I want to say yes so badly. " But", I qualified, "although I am flattered with your offer of marriage, I feel that things are moving too fast. Let's not do something that we will regret and hurt each other irrevocably, spoiling something sacred and profane, spoil

He appeared downcast and questioned how he would manage the suspense of 10 protracted days of waiting, obscuring the happiness that was so obvious on his face with lines of dread. He appeared despondent as I tried to persuade him that, while I could never imagine leaving this area, which was like heaven to me, and did not want to tie him down, he had his entire life ahead of him.

In addition, because I was an older woman, I would probably be perceived as a seductress, cradle thief, and man-eater. Although I couldn't give a damn what the world thought, I didn't want him to suffer because he would undoubtedly do so due to the insults directed at me rather than for himself.

CHAPTER 16

I needed to do something to lift his spirits because he was looking so dejected. As our class came to a close, I asked him if he would want to explore my legs by kneeling down and straightening them for a better view. He covered my smooth knees as well as my toned pins, spreading his mouth wide as I kicked back in return. He was a leg as well as a breast man.

He moved the towel to get a better view and then got bolder, reaching up my thigh before I swatted his hand away. I instructed him to lick the crease at the rear. Although I was aware that he was eager to see my cavern of divine delights, I was not yet prepared to reveal all of my riches.

He would have to settle with my calves and my toes, reverently sucking each one as he managed to hit all the right points, which made me groan with pleasure. He was practically groveling at my feet, learning from experience that went far beyond the pages of a book, and he asked me who I would like to be my Guru Dakshina. I responded that I was happy just seeing his smile, but if he wanted a massage later, it would be lovely if it pleased him.

He.

I gulped down my food quickly to get it over with and leave her wondering what had happened to me because I was ready and looking forward to the afternoon session, which promised to be eye opening for me. She explained to me that having sex was not a race to see who could finish first, but rather a marathon where you had to pace yourself to finish, and hurry frequently resulted in waste.

She took hold of my hand and rubbed it to make me feel better. My breathing got more labored, and it appeared that the opposite had happened. She placed my palm on her chest to feel her heartbeat and help me time my breath with hers after realizing this was ineffective, but I could feel her heart racing.

Her swollen nipples stiffened as my chilly palm touched them, and she breathed as shallowly as I did. She laughed since it was the exact opposite of what she had hoped to accomplish. She said that I was a bad influence and that I was causing disorder in her otherwise orderly life.

As she started her session, we moved to the living room and sat on the sofa. I was ready to listen and eager to both learn and be pleased. My thoughts raced with the possibility of gaining some practical experience in a field where it was desperately lacking when she said the session would take the form of a game of truth or dare.

She asked me a question to get me talking, see how much I knew, and show that it wasn't just a one-way conversation. I felt ashamed of my ignorance, but she was unfazed and even delighted that I was a clean slate without any preconceived ideas. She gave me the reassurance that I would graduate at the top of my class because she recognized my potential.

Now that it was my chance, I timidly asked her if she would teach me how to kiss, partly expecting her to say no. Nevertheless, I had not anticipated how far she would go. She began by making me feel uncomfortable and hot. When I was about to give up in frustration, she started a lip lock, and I tried to imitate her movements. As her soft lips pressed against mine and her lovely tongue touched mine, a plethora of sensations overpowered me. I was feeling a little down as we broke up to gather our breath again, but I just didn't want to stop.

When it was her turn, she chose the truth by asking if I beat one out without giving it a second thought. My challenge came to a satisfying conclusion. She had to physically spell everything out for me since I didn't understand the phrases or the lingo, and my ears turned red with shame.

Every time I had a wet dream, an intense sense of shame had always overtaken me. Only this morning I awoke from a wonderful enactment where her naked body was conspicuously displayed in a sticky puddle. I berated myself for having such impure ideas, but the more I made an effort to suppress them, the more powerful they grew. I was worried she would think I was a pervert, but instead I shocked her with my innocence.

She volunteered to teach me how to relieve myself because I had no idea what I was doing. I could hardly wait for her to start. I looked away in embarrassment as she snatched my towel aside, exposing my entire body to her eyes. My stiff cock throbbed with longing as her gentle fingers massaged its length. When she carefully examined my belongings, I could see her eyes enlarge with excitement. Her unwavering gaze reminded me so much of the way I used to look at her.

Then, as she started stroking her tongue up and down, she moistened her lips in a seductive manner, sending a wave of anticipation through my entire body. I really wanted to close my eyes and unwind, but I couldn't help but watch in awe as her fingers worked their magic on my nether regions, giving them new life. The friction heated up as she picked up the pace, becoming a touch too warm for comfort. Even though I was dripping at the tip, my skin was too delicate and unaccustomed to such frantic movement, so it chafed.

I agreed without thinking twice to her offer of a tit fuck even though I had no idea what it included. I was a dog on a leash in her hands, and I would have accepted even if she had offered me a sip of poison. If her touching me was like heaven, then her exposing her cleavage while I adjusted my penis was like seventh heaven. She transported me to the regions of joy by enclosing my penis in her ruby lips as I lost control and surged.

I ejaculated my pent-up reserves into her exquisite mouth since I had never anticipated such an unexpected surprise. She sucked me dry while kissing me with her tongue. As my balls emptied out into her and I collapsed back, exhausted, my thoughts went blank from the overwhelming pleasure. I longingly regretted not finding this sooner because I couldn't think of anything that could have made me feel even somewhat this way, and even better, I had no guilt to carry around with me.

CHAPTER 17

She frequently did it, which astonished me when I asked if girls did it too. When she informed me that women could have several orgasms at once while males required time to recover, I admit I felt a little envy. She stood up and disclosed that she had enjoyed herself while I had my eyes closed, recovering from my first orgasm. My mouth was wide open in shock as she did this.

I couldn't believe it and berated myself for closing my eyes and missing out on this amazing opportunity. As she turned around and showed me a wet area on the towel's back where her leftover love potion was still visible, it didn't give me much solace. She invited me to taste it after I inhaled deeply of her earthy aroma. She ran away as I squeezed the towel, purposely pinching her bottom as some of her sticky liquid covered my palm.

I closed my eyes and focused on savoring her flavor as I licked my fingers until they were completely dry. Her sly admissions that the oohs and aahs she sang in the bathroom at the end of the song were actually her moans as she got off made me even more speechless.

I asked her to point out the erogenous zones for my reference because I had read that knowing where they are is crucial if you want to pleasure your partner. My eyes immediately landed on her groin when she stated I was staring at the most significant one. She shook her head incredulously and said it was all in my head, and it took me some time to process the significance of her statement.

She then went on to systematically demonstrate each of the key ones to me in practice. When we finally got it from the head to the waist, I was ready for another round and my pecker was back up. I was able to stay significantly longer than previously thanks to my past experience, but only for a short while because I quickly developed a new load.

She had placed her hand under her towel in the meantime, and within seconds it was wet once more. Her eyes were averted, and she groaned quietly as a fresh quantity of water poured across the towel's front from within. As she tasted her thick white cream, she took her fingers off and placed them next to her lips, licking them clean. She noticed that I was gazing intently at her, like a dog waiting for a bone, and asked if I would like some.

She simply dipped her hand into her reserves and scooped out a dollop of her salsa directly from the pot while I enthusiastically nodded, my throat parched. I closed my eyes to appreciate the nourishment while savoring her nuanced flavor, which was a little fruitier than before. She was happy with my response and enquired as to if I wanted more. In response to my request, she returned to the towel's folds and scooped out a fresh batch. I gulped it down with greed, forcing her to keep scrounging for more until her cove was emptied.

Yet, it had merely whetted my appetite, and I was hankering for more. She then did the next best thing by kissing me on the lips while she was seated on my lap. It gave me a taste of my own ample reserves, which I had generously given to her. As they combined with the leftovers of hers to form a potent cocktail, we both drank greedily and wildly while sharing them. My prick, energized by this sustenance, was ready for action once more and prodded the towel through her legs in search of her moist confines. She jumped to her feet quickly because she didn't want to escalate the situation and do something we would later regret.

The words "I love you" and "Will you marry me" were incidentally the same ones I had mouthed verbatim more than a decade earlier, and though the situation was obviously different, the essence was the same; they came naturally, straight from the heart. I was enthralled, got on my knees, looked into her deep brown eyes, and suddenly found myself mouthing those words.

I feared I had gone a little too far when I saw her eyes widen, but the words had already come out of my mouth. My trepidation soon gave way to unbridled excitement as I heard "I love you too." There was always a but to qualify, complicate, or add to a statement. She asked for 10 days so that we could both consider it. I didn't want to wait even 10 minutes, let alone 10 days. Despite the seemingly endless wait, I was relieved to have the phobia out of the way. She hadn't flatly rejected me, but she had expressed her thoughts in return. It was a modest beginning, but one that we could expand upon.

I gladly responded when she asked if I wanted to pick up where we left off because I was trying to take advantage of every opportunity that came my way. She had seen my wares up close, so I wanted a dekho from her as payment in exchange. She had yet to cross the ultimate boundary and tell me the truth, though. While kissing her knees, I still tried to steal a glance, but she swatted my hand away as I tried to lift the towel.

She was sexily sighing as I squeezed her toes, and as I pushed all the appropriate buttons, I could see the beginnings of an orgasm as she leaned her head back and squirmed. My heart was so full of appreciation that I questioned her about what I could gift at her lotus feet as Gurudakshina. She didn't have any requests, but if I felt up to it later tonight, she wouldn't mind a soothing massage.

All she wanted to do right now was take a quick shower to remove the dry residue left behind by her leaking cistern, which had caked her skin and left her feeling quite uneasy. I volunteered to help her by going with her to the restroom, but she turned around and gestured for me to go to my room instead.

I took a shower as well, not because I truly needed one but more to practice the method she had earlier shown. She suddenly started singing, fully aware that I was listening intently on the other end. "How are you feeling?" was asked to Janaab. From the other end, my response, "What do you think?" (Kya khayal hain aapka), was received with great understanding. I finished with "Yun hi phisal gaye ha ha ha" (That's why I slipped) after she sang "Tum to machal gaye ho ho ho" (You became fun).

While we were singing, I had the image of her getting into the shower naked, rivulets of water lapping over her warm, smooth skin. Her legs opened wide as she put a few fingers into her slit and began to move them in and out more quickly.

74

CHAPTER 18

Her large breasts, which were now pointedly erect, were being massaged by the other hand.

And I noticed that my hand was mimicking the method she had shown me earlier that day. When I sang the chorus, "Ah, ah ah Dipa," I noticed that my penis was throbbing, engorged, and slick as it pulsed out, sending forth ropes of a sticky thick white paste.

She knew what I was doing, but she never missed a chance to tease me and asked rhetorically why I spoke her name aloud. Also, she couldn't quite recall this chorus's final chorus being so lengthy. I provided as nice a response as I could, claiming that I was only practicing the moves she had taught me that morning and that repetition is the key to getting better at them.

She blushed and there was a long gap as I felt it through the wall. I questioned her as to why she had suddenly stopped talking. She laughed like a little girl and said, "Nothing, just thinking of you, polishing your technique, that's all." I smiled as I came out of the shower on my own. I went to the kitchen without putting on any clothes because she had already seen everything. I also had ten days to make my case, therefore I didn't want to waste any chances to do so.

She descended the stairs wearing the same white petticoat, but I could make out her damp hair dripping over her pendulous breasts and the outline of the groove between her thighs. I came up behind her, wrapped my arms around her, and fiddled with her breasts while she worked over the stove busy making the basic lunch of dal chawal and spicy potatoes that I had asked.

She met me halfway by pushing her bottom behind. She tried to shake me off as I was mesmerized by her, sounding furious. Her erect nipples, however, revealed a mismatch between her words and her actions. When I attempted to reach inside her petticoat, I was met with slivers of smooth flesh. She swatted my hand away and told me I had grown extremely bad and was taking too many liberties as I reached below for another slit.

The supper was ready, and because we were so famished from all the sexual activity, we devoured it quickly while keeping to ourselves. After finishing, we headed to the lounge to unwind as our bellies groaned. Then, the phone rang. It was my mother on the phone when she answered the strangely quiet phone and handed it to me.

My mother, who had a keen antenna, knew something was wrong and chastised me for bothering her. I struggled to control my smile because she had no idea who was bothering whom. I could not contain my happiness as I professed my love for her and my desire to wed her. My mother was a good place to start because I was very verbose and wanted to shout it from the rooftops.

She commented that she had a sneaking suspicion that this would happen, but not this quickly, since she could tell that I was elated. She was ecstatic for both her and me. She insisted on knowing every graphic detail, so I gave in while neatly omitting the erotic portions. She enquired as to whether I had made a proposal and what Dipa's response was.

I informed her that I didn't have a response yet and that she should think about it. Mom pleaded with me to be patient, but she was sure that I should give her some time and space because she would get a good reaction. Mom claimed that she almost forgot to disclose the reason she had phoned because of how happy she was to hear the wonderful news. The prime minister declared a total lockdown for the following two weeks due to a virus outbreak that had reached our borders.

She pleaded with me to remain put and safe. I was more than willing to comply. She requested that I connect her with Dipa since she had had enough of my blathering and was ready to talk. Now that the situation had completely turned around, Dipa was the one answering inquiries with monosyllabic responses and a flush growing across her face.

As the conversation came to a conclusion, I was smiling and playing a broad, silly grin on my lips, like a displeased Cheshire cat. With family consent, the road to happiness was finally open with no speed bumps, and I couldn't control my joy. She gave me a delighted kiss as she expressed her relief at having the support of her family, which was important to her.

She shocked me with her initiative, but I don't look a gift horse in the mouth, so I matched her zeal and was happy to have released a significant burden as I tweaked her nips. We stopped and gasped for oxygen before starting again, this time slower, deeper, worry-free, and feeling as light as air.

I couldn't help but giggle, and she regarded me with interest. I expressed to her my gratitude that my mother had not placed a video call. If she had even the faintest inkling of the shenanigans we were up to, she would urge me to return right away, lock down be damned. She would be scandalized to see her well-hung son in the buff and her well-endowed daughter-in-law halfway there.

She smacked me in a fake outrage while grinning to herself and expressing her relief that her mother had been so forgiving. Even in her wildest dreams, she hadn't foreseen this change of events, thus her joy was overflowing. Not knowing how my mother would respond, I was relieved that she didn't find my revelation shocking. She did not object to the title of "daughter in law," which made me feel more confident about my chances of success despite my propensity to mess things up.

The night was still very early, and the day only seemed to keep getting better and better. She placed her head on my shoulders as we sat quietly, holding hands, and I was relishing the moment and didn't want it to end. We discussed our hopes, worries, and aspirations, and we were shocked by how well we could read each other's minds since we occasionally spoke the same things at the same moment, finishing each other's sentences.

We talked about the wonderful times we had as children, and I asked if I may sleep on her lap like I had done so many times before.

CHAPTER 19

She sat cross-legged and nodded as she raised her petticoat above her knees. This allowed me to see her beautiful thighs, smooth knees, and shapely calves. My cock grew once more as I struggled to see farther into the shadows because she saw what I was doing and wanted to avoid accidentally exposing her jewel box by pooling her petticoat between her thighs.

She rubbed her nipples against my cheek as I was lying on her lap, and I grabbed one to get my nightly dosage of milk. To help me relax, she rubbed my erection in the meanwhile. I was about to let go as her deft fingers enticed my cream out when she grabbed the head between her fingers to prevent me from spilling my seed and instead wanted to store it for later. She lowered her face to mine and gave me a passionate kiss as her curls once again covered our lips.

My hair felt damp, and I assumed she was wet as well because of the unmistakable aroma of her arousal. I kissed her again, this time on her lower lips, whose outlines I could see through the wet petticoat as our kiss ended. She wriggled under my insistent attention as I rotated my head around and focused on the moist region.

Yet I didn't give up on my focus, propelled by the groans coming from her mouth and her hands guiding my head while pulling at my hair. As her groans grew louder, I made excellent use of my tongue, lips, and teeth to detect a lump at the top of her slit that was extremely sensitive to my touch. I focused all of my attention on it.

The petticoat was now wet on both sides, from my saliva on the surface and the internal moisture. As she fell back and I savored her energizing tonic, I felt her body tense up beneath me and a stream of her potent cream pour out as she yelled out my name loudly.

As smaller waves erupted at regular intervals, I had just made her approach and have a female orgasm up close. After she was finished, I turned back to find her covered in sweat, shining in the moonlight, and taking deep breaths. She gave me a critical look, waved her finger in my face, and said that I was a bad boy for touching her without her consent and that I would undoubtedly face punishment in line with the seriousness of the offense. I made an attempt to act remorseful and begged for compassion through her good graces. She demanded that I give her the massage I had promised to give her that afternoon, but I was unable to sway her. If this was punishment, I would soon start breaking the law again. She.

Sex education was a nasty endeavor, both physically and figuratively. By the time it was over, I needed a shower at the very least because I was warm, wet, and sticky. He wanted to follow me as I went to the bathroom, and I was almost inclined to let him because of the delicious possibilities that this offered. Yet, his marriage proposal sent my world into a tailspin, and I needed to put some space between us so that I could think clearly.

The overwhelming mustiness of my dried juices attacked me as I shut the bathroom door; it gave me the impression that I was in a boudoir and made me want to touch myself once more. I entered the shower and started humming a tune; sure enough, he joined me for a duet. By the time we were done, he began to groan, and I blushed at the thought of him wanting to test my lessons so badly. I pictured him wiping one out while I reflexively reached for my nub to do the same. I was careful to be silent as I flicked my clit, biting my lip to keep from sighing as I opened my legs and visualized him ravishing me.

When I went to the kitchen with only a petticoat, I was shocked to see him waiting there with nothing but an erection. I hurried to the stove in the hope that cooking would cover up my flush. He massaged my breasts as he slid up to me, and I was pleasantly pleased to feel his erection nestle into my butt cheeks. He started to thrust against me, and I pushed back, encasing his hardness in the supple folds of my bottom.

I admonished him since it was difficult for me to focus on cooking, partly hoping he would stop and half wanting him to keep talking. He complied with my requests. I pushed his fingers away as they attempted to enter the opening in my petticoat. I was aware that our passions would get out of hand if he got close to my wet slit.

After our exertions earlier that afternoon, we fed each other in quiet while we were starving. We overindulged to the point where we sagged on the couch in the living room like beached whales and regretted it. His mother was on the other end of the phone when it rang. I transferred the phone to him since I was so terrified and had no idea what to say.

I quickly regretted it since he couldn't contain his joy and revealed everything, virtually all of it r-rated. By the time he was done, I was coyly blushing because I knew she wasn't crazy about me but was happy for us. Her enthusiasm was audible over the phone as she yearned to talk to me. On the other hand, I was rendered speechless by the unexpected turn of events, relieved beyond words, and my happiness.

She expressed her joy for both of us and urged me not to yield to pressure or hold back from punishing him if he disobeyed. She could sense my joy and praised my maturity for letting things develop naturally rather than rushing in. She informed us about the lockdown and urged us to be secure.

I felt relieved, and all of my anxieties regarding family approval vanished. While we just sat there relishing the moment, he was also in a good mood and cracking a few jokes. I had to pull up my petticoat to sit cross-legged since he asked if he could sleep on my lap with his eyes fixed on my thighs.

He fell asleep in my lap, and as I massaged his cheek and fluffed his hair, a tenderness came over me. It reminded me of all the times he insisted on sleeping in my lap while I read him a tale or sang him a lullaby while rocking him to sleep.

Yet, as his cock steadily rose against gravity in response to my charms, a fantasy of sorts was playing in my head instead of the story, as it doubtlessly was through his as well.

CHAPTER 20

My milk was flowing and I was sighing with pleasure as he nibbled at my nipples, just beyond the reach of his open lips.

Deeper down, my loins were also getting wetter, and through the thin fabric of my petticoat, I could smell my need. He turned around to take a deeper breath and top up his milkshake with some cream after realizing that he could. Through the wet fabric of my petticoat, his lips found my lower ones and molded themselves around mine. I gasped as his tongue pushed within my fissure, and met with my sensitive nub.

For his first effort at eating pussy, without any obvious training he was doing an admirable job, as I squirmed, seeking to maximize the exquisite sensations that rushed through me. He attacked my treasure cove with a relentless vigor, and when I was primed and prepared for release, I gently pulled at his hair to encourage him to stop as well as carefully steered him in the appropriate direction.

My floodgates opened with a shout, and waves of ecstasy swept over me as I closed my eyes and tilted my head back, giving him the full amount of my jamba juice and relinquishing control of my body. Despite his best attempts to suck up the last of my manna, my petticoat was now actually dripping.

I retrieved a half-apron from the kitchen and asked him if the offer for a massage was still valid because I didn't want to squander my valuable fluid. He asked me which oil he could use, and he was eager and willing to do so. I just removed my petticoat, the half apron protecting my modesty from his intense gaze. I then took the enormous bowl of flowers that had been set up on the coffee table and wrung my petticoat dry as all of my liquids dripped into it.

As I sat down on the mat and gave him his first panoramic view of my behind, it would have to do for the time being. He immediately began to work, rubbing all the stress out of my neck, back, and clavicles with the help of his digits. I was purring in pleasure as he stroked my skin with his fingers because it felt so amazing.

Every rib was precisely traced as he worked meticulously down my back, and the aroma of the flowers combined with my own juices created an entrancing atmosphere. My hands were groping his cock, which also required a massage, when he yanked them back and stretched them out. Meanwhile, his hands began stroking my breasts as they rose up in front of him. As soon as his balls emptied, he began to throb between my fingers and shoot white lines up my back.

I instructed him to finish utilizing this fluid before it dried, and he surprised me by doing so. His weight allowed me to entirely relax, but one part of him was still at work pushing into my buttocks and between my thighs as he bobbed up and down, hard again in need of release. I asked him to pinch the head to limit the flow just as he was ready to lose control once more and I clamped my thighs like a vice around it to stop a disaster.

He then enjoyed playing with my springy buttocks' soft smoothness before I tightened up as I felt a finger poke into my a**hole. At first, I backed away instinctively, but as I felt a familiar wetness leak out of my pussy, rising them slightly to meet his penetrating digit, I began to love the fresh sensations. Then, as I hooked a finger into my cove to clear out the leftovers of my cum, he retracted his finger and took a deep sniff of my fecal odor. I urged him to use his tongue to clean me up because the massage fluid was now caked to my back. He licked me clean, giving close attention to my erogenous areas as he went. He was so skilled at it that I felt like I was melting in his hands. Afterwards, he stooped lower and began a series of nips right below my buttocks, separating my thighs in the process. He managed to get his tongue into my slit as well as stick his head into the opening to taste the liquids that had collected down my apron.

He had cunningly managed to break my last defense from behind, hidden as it was from the front, before I realized what had happened. I quickly pulled my thighs back together, but not before he swiped my cream on his hands. As much as I regretted shutting them, I knew his persistent attack on my fortifications would soon breach my walls, and at this pace I wouldn't survive even past tonight. It felt fantastic to feel a male's touch on my pussy again.

I was in rapture once again by the time he finished kissing my toes after sliding down to my knees and thighs. He flipped me over, putting us face to face. When I saw his dick working full tilt and sparkling with fluids oozing out of him, I licked my lips hungrily.

Being in full flow myself, I wasn't doing too poorly, and I placed the petticoat under my thighs to catch the overflow.

He was behind me, giving me the luxury of closing my eyes. With the visual delight in front of me, it was now difficult to even blink an eyelid. He began at my toes and worked his way up, quickly dispatching my calves as a continual stream of gasps naturally came from my mouth.

He tried to peep under the apron once he reached my knees, but his line of sight was obstructed by the petticoat that was positioned beneath my thighs. He cautiously placed his hands under the apron as he cautiously climbed up my thighs, fearing that if he became too fresh, I would end the session in advance.

I had already gone too far down the trail to care and wouldn't have even noticed if he tore the apron off. But until I explicitly approved of his behavior, his upbringing prevented him from doing anything that had previously been outside the rules for him. Furthermore, he was too respectful to even consider asking. His hands continued to massage as they warmed up as they approached my mound.

My stubble was only starting to show up here and there as I touched its smooth surface and felt the texture. To give him access to my warm, moist core, I opened my thighs as widely as I could. He cautiously dipped one finger, then another, while using his other hand to touch the top of my clit.

CHAPTER 21

I told him to bend his fingers just a little to heighten the pleasure I was experiencing and scoop out my cream as my sighs had turned into moans and I was on the verge of an orgasm. I also signaled for him to lie on top of me and kiss me. With a whoop, I arrived as his mouth touched mine, trembling as I used all of my reserves and crossing my legs behind his back to buckle under the impact of the pleasure.

We lay there satisfied in each other's embrace, relishing the joy, when he came too and sprayed white sticky ropes across my tummy meeting my breasts. He didn't know what hit him. He attempted to move over as his weight was pressing down on me but the cum had us attached to one another and I was now on top. I took a break, admiring the strong muscles that supported my gentle contours. My skin was sensitive, and his chest hair was tightly matted, so each attempt to stand up caused pain for both of us. I couldn't help but laugh out loud at the absurdity of the scenario. Then, out of compassion for him, I requested him to use his hands to break up the caked-on come by milking my breasts. He complied, at first with joy and later, as we started to separate, a little wistfully, wishing we might remain together forever.

I looked at the mess—on our body as well as the couch—and realized that we needed to clean up before calling it a day. He offered to clean the living room while I went into the kitchen to clean the stained apron, put on the still-wet petticoat, and led him up the stairs like my little lamb. He attempted to escape my hold as I dragged him in as I opened the door to my room to use the restroom.

He didn't have to respond when I inquired whether he was too shy to allow me bathe him like before. He appeared to have won the lottery from the look on his face, which said it all. I explained that there was a bathtub there that would make it simpler to clean, but judging by the look he gave me, he didn't agree with me.

I questioned him about his preference for hot or cold water as I ran the bath. He claimed that he liked it to steam like I do. Under the avalanche of his compliments, I could only blush. He entered the tub, half expecting me to strip off and join him in the tub, but I only partially obliged, keeping the petticoat on. His eyes opened as he could see every feature as clearly as day as it stuck to my figure, silhouette defining all the curves, but the water soon turned it translucent.

I immediately saw how foolish it was to jump into the water, but there was no turning back; I had already gotten wet and was beginning to flush as his organ reared up above the placid surface. While I washed his body and properly cleaned him, he began humming.

Ek chatur naar karke singaar: "A brilliant woman is wonderfully decked up, she walks into the entrance of my heart, and kills me with her eyes." Mere Mann Ke Dwar Yeh Ghusat Jaat: "Hum Marat Jaat Arre Ae Ae Ae." A bright woman is exceedingly smart, he proceeded in the second verse: "Ek chatur naar badi hoshiyar,

Apne hi jaal mein phasat jaat, Hum hasat jaat arre ha ha ha." She sets up a trap for others, but she is caught in it herself.

He continued without skipping a beat with another song that offered him tit for tat, "Thande thande paani se nahana chaahiye,Gaana aaye ya naa aaye,Gaana chaahiye," and I was amazed at his perfect choice of words. One must try to sing even if they don't know the words.

He added, "Ek ladki bhigi bhagi si, Soti raaton mein jaagi si, Mili ek ajnabi se, Koi na age na peechhe, Tum hi kaho ye koi baat hai,"- "A girl out at night while everyone is asleep, no one in sight, I can't make any sense of it, can you?"

I was enjoying the chorus while also stroking his body. He was also having a ball making sure I was spotless by slipping his fingers into tight crevices and making me writhe in pain. I gave him the full benefit of my indulgence, teaching him how to lubricate himself with soap before a fight—not that I thought he would ever need it. His hands would be too busy tending to my needs and desires, and his organ would need as much rest as it could get since I might be a challenging customer.

He was mesmerized by the smoothness of my mound, so I explained that I preferred a Brazilian, preferred to keep my pubic hair free because it made me feel feminine and was also hygienic. I offered to cut the vegetation at the base of his penis and the bushes beneath his arms and advised him to keep his jungles under control. He leaped at my offer, but I declined, explaining that I was simply looking to unwind and that if he promised to behave, perhaps another time.

"Mein chali mein chali, dekho pyar ki gali, mujhe roko na koi, mein chali mein chali" — "I'm leaving, have had enough of love, please don't stop me, I'm going" — is the song I sang as I stood up to go. In response, he sang, "Abhi na jao chod kar, ki dil abhi bhara nahi," which roughly translates to, "Please don't go and leave me alone yet, my heart is not yet full." But as I fell backward into his prone body with a loud splash, he grabbed my hand and pulled me towards him.

And I experienced a profound, enduring love as I was held in the warm water by his arms while I laid there. After what seemed like a lifetime, I felt something rise up against my back. I was relieved that there was at least a flimsy petticoat between us since I knew that if I waited any longer, I wouldn't be able to contain myself. He began to object once more as I stood up once more, the water flowing off my moist skin. But I remained steadfast, displaying my tits at him and warning that if he lingered any longer, his stick would turn into a rope and my peaches into prunes from too much exposure. I immediately removed the petticoat and wrapped a towel over myself before entering the room and disappearing from view.

I had just finished putting on the first pair of pants I could find when he came out of the bathroom. I realized I was wearing a pair that left little to the imagination when I saw his wide-eyed gaze again since the fragile lace made my lips' outline very obvious.

CHAPTER 22

Nonetheless, after having seen everything there was to see, he continued to be completely enamored with my charms despite having seen everything there was to see.

I laughed tinklingly as I snapped my fingers across his face, jolting him back to reality. I said, "Good night," understanding that the longer he stayed, the harder it would be for me to restrain myself. He appeared dejected and had anticipated staying a little longer. He questioned, "Don't I deserve a goodnight kiss?" I promised to give him one if he wouldn't touch me. But I didn't drink my usual glass of milk at night.

He was right; if I didn't take care of it, my breasts would hurt. Thus, as he approached me in a daze, I sat down in the alcove close to the window, shimmering in the moonlight. I stroked his hair as he lowered his head to my breast and began hungrily draining them, one at a time. I surprised myself with my wantonness as I carelessly placed one hand on his cock and stroked it while placing the other inside the gusset of my pants.

My breasts were now completely dry, but liquids underneath the surface were just starting to percolate. I started to feel guilty for giving in to all of his requests and wished I had the courage to refuse. Knowing that I would miss him just as much as he would miss me, I leaned in for our final kiss of the evening. When our lips touched, his hands were indeed behind his back, as promised. Sometimes I hoped he wouldn't be such a gentleman and would take the initiative on his own instead of constantly deferring to me.

But, you can always find a flaw to your benefit. I could and would freely use my hands whatever I pleased. Our tongues twined and we continued to talk endlessly while I hungrily kissed him and cradled his head in my arms.

His eyes were still closed, relishing what was left as I stopped, my lips turning blue from heavy breathing. As he eventually opened them, I could feel tears still clinging to the edges and, shockingly, I had the same emotions. Even a word would trigger a collapse. He slowly withdrew himself from my embrace as my hands gripped the air, and loped off without so much as a sideways glance. I gazed out the window, my eyes hazy, focusing on the darkness.

As soon as he left, I snatched up the closest pillow and buried my face in it while sobbing profusely. I trembled to think what would happen when he ultimately had to say goodbye if just a small time of separation could cause such a powerful emotion. My bed felt incredibly empty, and it was making me feel really depressed.

I went outside to the hallway, took off my pants, grabbed his singlet, and got a deep sniff of his masculine aroma while my hand searched for my hole. I pressed my ear to the wall because I believed I heard a noise. And I continuously heard "ah, ah, ah."

I'm sure he had the same notion, and now that I think about it, I don't remember leaving my petticoat on the line. I enjoyed matching my heartbeat to his. And as I got closer to my goal, I heard him calling my name. I yelled his name aloud in an effort to reach him as it sparked my own climax. I held the pillow tight against my thighs and let myself to experience wonderful fantasies of ecstasy.

We talked about it again and again. But this time I was convinced that he meant what he was saying. And I thought about it for days thinking to let our family know about our relationship. I was scared at first but along the line we had our family support and we were told to perform the marriage rites.

It was a huge ceremony and we became the talk of town , Everyone in the community attended our ceremony and we became the happiest couples.

THE END

CPSIA information can be obtained
at www.ICGtesting.com
Printed in the USA
BVHW031407200423
662563BV00035B/7

9 781804 347799